# Big Bad Killing Machine

**By Sally A Allen**

## Chapter 1

From the get go Colton Colby was a big boy. His mother had gained fifty pounds before he was born and he weighed in at ten pounds five ounces. He possessed large hands and feet and had a short, broad neck. His hair was straight and black.

When he was teething, his father called him Cutter and the name struck with him all his life.

When Colton was two, he acquired a mean streak and hollered constantly at his parents. Katy and Drew didn't know what to do with him. Since he was their first child, they didn't realize he was different from most boys his age.

At fourteen, he had developed into the class bully. Alvin, a quiet scholarly boy, became fast friends with Colton, even though they were from different worlds.

Colton came home and put his backpack on the table. "What on earth happened to your bag? There's blood on it!" Katy exclaimed.

"That's just red clay. We live in Georgia, you know," he replied innocently.

Katy lifted the backpack up and inspected it. "Colton, stop lying, this is blood. Sit down and tell me what happened."

"Kenny started a fight," he answered belligerently.

"Why don't I believe you?"

"He jumped in a puddle and splashed me with water. Look, my pants and shirt are all drenched!"

"Did you hit him?"

"Yeah, he deserved it."

"Couldn't you have just splashed him back? He's much smaller than you."

"His crowd was coming after me. I wanted to finish him off."

"Did you hurt him?"

"I think I broke his nose," Colton said smugly.

"Oh dear, now Kenny's father is going to give you detention. Doug is the principal, remember?"

"Kenny's a spoiled brat. Someone should have clocked him before this!"

Katy lost her temper. "You will call Kenny and apologize right now!"

Colton groused, but went to the phone and dialed the number. He came back looking smug. "He wasn't home. His mother said his dad took him to the hospital."

"Great! Get up to your room! Wait until your father hears about this!"

Colton stomped upstairs and soon Katy could hear a heavy metal band screeching from his speakers.

Buck, the family Shepard, followed Cutter up the stairs. Before long, Katy heard a yelp and the dog came running back down. She knew Colton had kicked the dog in his fury.

"Come here, boy," Katy said and patted his head. She went over and opened the door. "Go outside and chase squirrels."

Buck gratefully ran outside, happy to get as far away from Colton as possible.

Katy was in tears when Drew got home. "What happened?" he asked.

She blurted out the whole story and Drew immediately went to the phone and called Doug Larson. He apologized for Cutter's behavior, but Doug wouldn't have any of it.

"Colton is going to get detention and if he gets in any more trouble, he'll be suspended. Colton broke Kenny's nose; that's unacceptable!" he slammed down the phone in Drew's ear.

Drew was seething. "I'm going upstairs and teach Cutter a lesson," he told Katy.

When he came back downstairs, he held Colton's cell phone. "He was on the phone complaining to Alvin, but I jerked it away from him and told him I'd return it when I was good and ready."

Katy looked like she was going to cry again, so Drew took her in his arms. "Just give him a little time, he'll straighten out."

"Sometimes I doubt it," she replied, shaking all over. "Are all adolescent boys like that?"

"I was," Drew admitted.

"Well bully for you. I guess he's a chip off the old block."

"Not exactly, I never picked a fight with anyone."

"Good," Katy said and prepared a dinner neither one of them ate.

After Colton had finished his punishment, he calmed down and even got better grades. He was now maintaining a C average. Katy and Drew sighed with relief. Maybe he had finally learned his lesson and would behave himself from now on.

## Chapter 2

Larry Gill, the football coach, heard about Colton's problem and decided it would be good for him to join the football team. That way he could take out his frustration on the field. Because of his size, he started him out as a linebacker.

"Guess what?" Colton said happily to his parents. "I'm going to play football on the junior varsity this year!"

Drew and Katy were thrilled. "Cutter's finally participating in extracurricular activities," his father said proudly.

"Thank God," Katy replied.

When Colton went to pick up his uniform, Coach Gill welcomed him to the team and asked him to sit down. "Colton, I want to advise you of a few rules members of our football team must follow. First, you must keep your grades at a C average or better. Next, we require that you be in bed by eleven o'clock the night before a game. If you do well, you'll automatically be on the first team in high school. I have faith in you, so I'll see you at practice after school on Monday."

The first football game was against the Bronson Chargers, an old rival team from a school about thirty miles away. It was a tradition to play for the old river jug. The winning team was given the jug, with much fanfare, until the next season.

Drew and Katy arrived at the game early; they didn't want to miss a minute of Colton's first game. When the players walked out on the field, it was evident that he was bigger than anyone else on the team. "Cutter looks like a giant wrapped up in red and white," Drew joked.

Katy pretended to be offended. "Stop it; you're talking about my first born."

The band played the national anthem and the team stood at attention with their helmets held over their hearts. The referee's whistle blew and the game began.

On the first play from scrimmage, an offensive player from Bronson tried to run through a hole in Westfield's line. Colton quickly filled the gap and tackled the runner from behind. He caught the player in the legs and dumped him heavily to the ground for a three yard loss. The fans in the stands went wild, cheering and waving red and white flags.

On the next play, Bronson's quarterback threw a pass that sailed over Colton's head. He turned around and roughly tackled the intended receiver. The boy was slow getting up, but the crowd started clapping and chanting Colton's name.

Katy's eyes sparkled. "Listen, Drew, they're rooting for our son!"

"I know it's great, honey, but remember it's only a game."

"What do you mean?"

"Sports are supposed to teach the boys some sportsmanship and help them make the right decisions in life. I only hope Cutter leaves his fighting on the football field and behaves himself everywhere else."

Katy looked at Drew smiling. "My boy will be just fine," she said.

After the game, Colton became instantly popular; all the girls were seeking his attention. Although he had never seriously thought about girls, one cheerleader with long blonde hair caught his fancy. He made it a point to pass her in the hall as much as possible. When homecoming was approaching, he asked her to go to the dance with him.

"I'd love to!" she squealed, batting her big blue eyes at him.

"Cool," he replied. "Do you want to go to a movie this weekend?"

"Oh wow, I'd really like that!" She fumbled in her purse and found a pen and paper. She quickly wrote down her phone number and handed it to him. "I have to go or I'll be late for class," she said and ran down the hall.

Colton sighed with satisfaction. He knew she was an airhead, but her parents were rich and she was beautiful.

Alvin became interested in a plain girl with braces. She was on the honor roll, just like him. One day, he and Colton were walking home from school. "Hey, man, guess what? Lynda Brown and I decided to go steady!" he said excitedly.

"No shit!" Colton exclaimed, wondering what he saw in the plain girl.

"She's the smartest girl I've even met. She gets straight A's and runs circles around everyone in our computer class."

"If she's so smart, why is she dating you?" Colton joked.

Alvin couldn't see the humor in it. He replied haughtily, "We have the same interests and enjoy studying together."

"Well, I have news for you too. Sexy Morgan Miller and I are going to the movies this weekend."

"Why do you want to hang around her and her snotty friends? They all think their shit doesn't stink."

Colton looked at him and stated, "If you got to know her, you'd love her. She has a terrific personality."

"Plus big boobs and shapely legs," Alvin mocked.

"Nothing wrong with that, is there? I like my girls wrapped up in a pretty package. Say, why don't you and Lynda join us Saturday? We'll have a blast!"

Alvin considered. "Lynda wouldn't go for it, she hates all those girls."

"She should get to know them, maybe she'd change her mind."

"Okay, Cutter, I'll ask her and let you know."

"Talk to you later," Colton said, turning into his driveway.

After school the next day, he was stashing his books in his locker when Morgan walked by arm in arm with Greg Matthews, the quarterback of the football team. A siege of jealousy overtook him and his anger flared. What did they think they were doing?

He got even angrier when Alvin called him. Lynda had overheard Morgan and her friends laughing about what a sucker Colton was, thinking Morgan was really interested in him. She had been dating Greg Matthews exclusively for over a year. Morgan had made a bet with the girls that she could wrap Colton around her finger at the drop of a hat.

Colton's face grew red with embarrassment. He vowed to make both Morgan and Greg pay. No one played him for a sucker!

Colton got his revenge the next day at practice. Greg was throwing the ball to his favorite receiver when Colton charged the boy before he could catch the ball. He tackled him hard and the boy went down clutching his leg.

The coach and his assistant ran over to the sobbing boy. Carefully, they checked his leg. "Oh my God, it's broken!" Coach Gill cried. "We've just lost our best receiver for the rest of the season!"

He glared at Colton. "What did you think you were doing?" he shouted.

Colton looked him in the eye and said, "I was practicing my moves just like you told me to, Coach. You said 'hit them as hard as you can'."

"I meant the opposing team, not ours, you jerk! I'm putting you on the bench indefinitely!"

Colton took off his helmet and walked off the field. *Revenge certainly comes with a price,* he thought. Then he remembered the look of shock on Greg's face and decided it was worth it. Who would he throw the football to now?

## Chapter 3

Morgan rushed up to Colton after school the next day. "What did you think you were doing yesterday?" she screamed.

"I was just doing what the coach told me to do," he replied, not looking her in the eye.

"Now we'll never win the championship," she said.

"So what? We've lost before. I know all you wanted was for Greg to be MVP this year."

"Is that why you did it?"

"Of course not, stupid. By the way, I heard you made a bet with that haughty group of yours. I'm standing here with egg all over my face."

Morgan blushed and looked down at the floor. "I'm sorry," she said quietly.

"Let's take a walk and let off some steam."

Morgan considered. "Okay, just to clear the air. Where should we go?"

"Let's take the trail leading to the quarry. It's quiet there and no one will bother us."

"Okay, let me put my books in my locker and we'll be on our way."

When she returned, Colton took her by the arm. "It's a wonderful day for a walk." He looked up and down the hallway and saw it was empty. "Come on, let's go," he urged.

The two of them walked through the woods, laughing and talking. When they reached the quarry, they stopped for a moment to look at the deep hole of water. "They say the water here is a hundred feet deep," Carlton said.

Morgan peered over the edge. "It scares me just to look at it."

"I thought we might go skinny dipping," Colton joked.

Morgan turned to look at him and he shoved her playfully.  She slipped and fell, hitting her head on a rock.

Colton fell to his knees and looked at her with distain.  Her eyes fluttered open and she cried, ""I'm hurt, Colton, take me home."

Instead, he grabbed a loose stone lying by the path.  Without hesitation, he threw it as hard as he could and it hit her in the forehead.

Morgan's eyes flew open, then lost their luster.

Colton stood transfixed and watched the life drain out of her.  She twitched once, and then she was still.

A mirage of feelings swept over him and he felt a sexual release.  Colton unzipped his pants and ejaculated on Morgan's body.  When he was finished, he coolly rolled her body into the quarry.

Feeling no remorse, he watched her body sink.  He turned around and jogged back to the start of the trail.  He looked around, but didn't see anyone.

It took him a half hour to get back to his house.  Colton ate a ravenous dinner and went to bed early.  He dreamed of how sensual he felt as he watched Morgan die.  The feeling overtook him again and his semen squirted into his pajama bottoms.  He didn't think he would experience such a high again in his lifetime.

# Chapter 4

Morgan's disappearance was the talk of Westfield. The police chief's office was flooded with calls from people who thought they saw her in one place or the other. Each call was checked out and all were proved false.

Morgan's parents were interviewed and they said the last time they saw Morgan she had been in the company of Greg Matthews.

The police showed up at football practice to question Greg. "Let's go sit on the bleachers," one officer said. "We have some questions we want to ask you."

Greg nodded glumly.

After they were seated, Officer Wade asked, "When did you last see Morgan Miller?"

Greg had tears in his eyes. "Yesterday after school. We talked about going to the concert in the park tonight."

"Were you in the habit of speaking to her every day?"

"Of course, she was my girlfriend!" Greg exclaimed.

Officer Gross looked him in the eyes. "You said 'was', past tense. Do you know something about her disappearance?"

Greg choked up. "May I use my cell phone to call my father?" he asked in a shaky voice.

Officer Wade nodded his head, thinking what a loud mouthed jerk John Matthews was. He thought because he owned the local department store, he could lord it over everyone in town.

A half hour after Greg's call a blue Cadillac pulled up to the football field. John Matthews and his attorney, Steve Wheeler, got out.

"Hold it right there!" Wheeler shouted. He looked at Greg. "Don't answer any questions without me present."

"Leave my boy alone!" Matthews shouted. "He feels bad enough that Morgan's missing. You're barking up the wrong tree if you think Greg had anything to do with it!"

"Listen here, John, we never said Greg had anything to do with Morgan's plight," Officer Wade said gruffly. "In fact, you can take him home with you; just don't let him leave Westfield unless you okay it with us."

"Greg has to go out of town with the football team. We have a chance to win the championship you know."

"I wonder what the cheerleaders will do without their captain," Wade said, looking sternly at Greg.

Greg burst into tears.

"Leave him alone!" his father shouted. "I'll call the chief!"

"Go ahead and do that," Wade said dryly. "I can't wait to see the look on your face when he tells you to go to hell."

## Chapter 5

Coach Gill called Cutter into his office the next day. "You have a killer instinct," Larry began.

*Good God,* Cutter thought, *they must have found the body already.*

The coach went on, "It's obvious you're a big, mean, tackling machine, but you're too rough for junior varsity. I'll let you finish out the year if you keep yourself under control." He looked at Colton sternly and shook his finger at him. "If you can manage to do that and get your grades up to a B average, I'll see that you're first string in high school next year."

"Thanks Coach," he said, relieved that the talk was only about football. "I'll do my best!"

"You're welcome. Now get out of here, I have work to do."

Colton left the coach's office elated and didn't watch where he was going. He collided with Patsy Smart and grabbed her to keep her from falling. His hand touched her generous breast and he found himself aroused. "I'm sorry, babe, I wasn't looking where I was going," he said.

"That's okay," she purred. "Just don't tackle me like you did Rob the other day."

Colton realized the act had somehow elevated him in her eyes. "I would never hurt a girl," he lied. "They're like cream puffs, tasty and sweet."

Patsy laughed. "You're so cool," she said.

Colton's face flushed with embarrassment and he blurted out, "Would you want to go to the homecoming dance with me?"

Patsy giggled. "I thought you'd never ask. I thought you were sweet on Morgan, but I guess I was wrong."

Colton's heart sank. Did she think he had something to do with her disappearance? "Why would you say that?" he asked.

"There were rumors you asked her out. Besides, I saw you walking with her after school."

Cutter thought fast. "I walked her part of the way home. We were just friends."

"I know, I was just teasing you."

Colton took her hand and pressed it to his lips. "Gotta go, hon, I'll see you tomorrow."

"Awesome," Patsy said, winking at him.

Colton wanted to run away from her, but he forced himself to walk slowly.

When he got home, his mother greeted him warmly. It seemed he could do no wrong since he had become the hero of the football team. She thought he was following in his father's footsteps. He played linebacker for Westfield quite a few years back.

"Hi, Mom," Colton said, forcing a smile. "What time is dinner?"

"It will be a while. I had a quilting bee with my club today, so I'm running late."

"Good, I thought I'd take Buck for a walk, he needs the exercise."

In reality, he wanted to revisit the scene of the crime. He was afraid Morgan's body would be floating in the quarry and wanted to make sure it wasn't.

Colton got the creeps following the same trail he and Morgan had walked not very long ago, but Buck tugged at the leash, pulling him forward.

When they got to the quarry, his and Morgan's footsteps would still be seen in the mud by the water. Buck sniffed them, obviously smelling Colton. *I have to get rid of those!* Colton thought, panicking.

He slipped the end of the dog's leash around a small tree and then picked up a rock and scoured the mud, erasing the footprints. To make sure they were gone, he took a tree branch and roughed up the ground.

Remembering why they had come to the quarry, he scanned the water and saw nothing. There wasn't a ripple.

Colton sighed with relief. *I don't have anything to worry about,* he thought. *I actually got away with murder!*

## Chapter 6

When he returned from his walk, Alvin slipped through the hedge between the two houses. "Hi, old buddy," Cutter said. "Come and sit on the steps."

"What's up with you?" Alvin asked. "I haven't seen you forever. Since you started playing football, you seem like a different guy altogether."

Colton gave him a playful punch on the arm. "Are you kidding? I'm the same person I always was." *Sure I am,* he thought. *Now I'm a felon headed for thirty years to life.*

"Sorry to hear about Morgan. What do you think happened to her?"

"I don't know. Maybe things got too rough for her and she took off. I don't want to talk about her; I have something to ask you. I need to pick my grades up. Do you think you could tutor me?"

"Is this about football?"

"Yeah, I have to maintain a B average if I want to play varsity next year."

"I could help you Saturdays and Sundays, but I got myself a part-time job after school during the week."

"Good for you. Saturdays and Sundays would help me out a lot."

They shook on it, glad they were going to be spending some time together.

On his way to football practice, Colton stopped by his locker to drop off his books. The hall was empty except for one couple. Colton couldn't believe it when he realized it was Patsy and Greg locked in an embrace. She was kissing him and rubbing her body against him. *What a slut,* he thought. *I'll show her.*

He slammed the locker as hard as he could, causing Greg and Pasty to jump apart. Colton gave them a knowing smile and left them staring after him.

*Well, there goes my homecoming date,* he thought. *I should kill her like I did Morgan.* He decided it was too soon to kill again. He longed for the next opportunity to present itself because he couldn't wait to feel that high again.

## Chapter 7

Frustrated, Cutter threw himself into football. He tackled harder and harder until most of the team was afraid to get in his way.

On the night of the homecoming game, Colton was obsessed with the need to hurt someone. In the fourth quarter, the opposing team was leading by three points. There was only one minute left on the clock.

The Bayshore quarterback was ready to throw the ball when Colton saw his opportunity. He dug in and took off, dodging players until he burst through the opposing line and launched himself at the quarterback. He pushed the boy roughly in the chest, causing him to fall backward and hit the ground with a resounding crack. His helmet flew off and he lay there dazed.

Upon contact, the football launched in the air and one of Colton's teammates grabbed it. Both teams watched as Westfield's tight end scrambled forty yards for a touchdown.

The team surrounded Colton and the cheering squad jumped in the air in ecstasy. The crowd shouted and clapped. No one noticed that Bayshore's quarterback was still lying on the field not moving.

When the ambulance siren wailed as it approached the field, the crowd grew silent.

The EMS team placed the injured player on a stretcher and put a neck brace on him. They carried him off the field and into the ambulance.

The Westfield team filed quietly off the field while the Bayshore team shouted obscenities at them. The two coaches huddled together, talking loudly. The spectators quietly left the stadium, the win spoiled by a tragic end.

Little did they know that Colton was secretly laughing. He hoped he killed the guy. His frustration was completely gone.

The headline in the newspaper the next day read "Westfield Defeats Bayshore 27-24!" A smaller headline read "Bayshore Quarterback Suffers Severe Concussion". The football crazed town didn't care how Westfield won the game, just as long as they won.

The next morning, Colton couldn't wait to get to school and revel in the attention he'd receive. At breakfast, Katy asked sadly, "Cutter, did you have to tackle that boy so hard?"

Drew broke in, "That's the name of the game. Football's not for weaklings."

"It seems like a game for barbarians," Katy replied. She looked at Colton. "You have to go to the hospital to see the boy."

Colton felt his euphoria drain out of him. He shook his head no.

"Leave him alone, Katy," he said. "Give him some time to absorb what happened. I know he'll do the right thing."

Colton clenched his fists. The frustration was back stronger than ever and he knew there was only one way to cure it. He would look for his second victim at once.

## Chapter 8

When he got home from school, he went upstairs to his parents' bedroom. He began opening dresser drawers and searching through them. He hit pay dirt when he opened the drawer of the nightstand. A package of his father's condoms was lying in plain sight. There was only one remaining. Quickly, he stuffed it in the pocket of his jeans.

He heard his mother's footsteps coming up the stairs so he quickly closed the drawer and ran to the closet. He made like he was trying to lift a box off the shelf.

"What are you doing in here?" his mother asked.

"I was looking for the old pictures of Dad in his football uniform."

"Colton, you know they're downstairs in the den."

He tried to put a surprised look on his face. "Of course they are, Mom, I'll go down and find them."

When Drew got home, Katy relayed the story, adding that she didn't believe Cutter's excuse.

Drew stood up, seemingly ignoring her and said, "I'm going upstairs and change out of my work clothes. We'll talk more when I get back."

When he walked in his bedroom, Drew went immediately to the nightstand. He smiled when he saw the empty condom box. *It's about time Cutter had his first taste of sex,* he thought. *I was younger than he is now.*

He decided not to mention it to Katy since she wouldn't understand. To her, Cutter was still her baby boy.

## Chapter 9

Saturday was Colton's tutoring session with Alvin. He arrived late and found him and Lynda passing the time while they waited for him. They were talking about the homecoming dance. "We looked for you, Cutter. Everyone was asking where the hero of the football team was."

"I didn't feel well," Colton lied. "I didn't want to go after what happened to Bayshore's quarterback."

"It wasn't your fault!" Lynda cried. "That's the way football goes."

"I guess," he said. He looked her over with new respect. Sure, she was plain with mousy brown hair and braces, but she possessed a certain something about her. Suddenly, he could see what Alvin saw in her.

Although Colton's mind wasn't on it, they got through his algebra lesson.

"That's it for the day," Alvin declared. "It's almost dusk and I want to walk Lynda home."

"No, you won't," she replied. "I'm a big girl and I can get home before dark."

"Okay," Alvin relented.

"Well," Colton said. "I have to get going. I'll see ya'll later." He grabbed his jacket and walked out the door. Instead of going home, he hid in the shadows across the street.

When Lynda walked out of Alvin's house, he made his move. "Hey," he said to her.

"What are you doing out here?"

"I just came back from taking Buck for a walk and saw you leaving Alvin's." He looked around. "It's getting dark; I don't think you should walk through that trail alone. Why don't I walk with you?"

Lynda hesitated, but was grateful for the offer. "Sure, come on," she replied.

They walked together silently, enjoying the cool autumn night. "Good thing you're wearing that scarf around your neck," Colton said.

"Yes, it's only silk, but it does protect my neck from the chill."

Colton stopped and put a hand on her arm. "Let me touch it. It looks so soft."

Lynda laughed. "It's just an ordinary scarf."

Colton quickly stripped it from her neck and sniffed it. Her scent lingered on it. He thought briefly about Alvin before he made his next move, but Colton couldn't help himself.

When Lynda began walking, he crept up behind her and pulled the scarf around her neck. She fell to the ground and stared up at him. "What are you doing, Colton? This isn't funny!"

"It's not supposed to be," he said menacingly.

Suddenly, Lynda realized what Colton intended to do. "Please don't," she begged.

"Shut up!" he exclaimed and hit her on the head.

Lynda gave a soft moan and tried to get away from him. Colton pulled the scarf tighter and she struggled to insert her hand between the scarf and her neck.

He turned her over roughly until she was flat on her back. Her eyes widened in fear. He stepped back and unzipped his fly. He reached in the pocket of his jeans and worked the condom over his penis. Lynda watched him, shaking violently. "If that's all you want, I'm willing to give it to you," she begged.

Colton didn't answer, but laid on her and pulled the scarf tighter. Lynda's eyes bulged and she made a choking sound. Colton wiggled against her body and kissed her on the lips, forcing his tongue between her teeth. She tried to turn her face away from him, but he only pulled the scarf tighter. Apparently, she gave up to her fate and her body went limp.

Colton pulled down her pants and roughly entered her, giving the scarf one final pull. Her eyes flickered and died as he climaxed within her. When he was finished, he placed his hand on her throat to check for a pulse. Satisfied that she was dead, he rearranged his clothes and looked down at her body, wondering what to do with it. He decided to leave it where it was. After all, anyone could have jumped her in the dark section on the trail. He tied the end of the used condom and disposed of it at Sully's Point where lovers often parked.

The following afternoon, Colton still hadn't heard of anyone finding Lynda's body. He felt removed from the situation, like he had never been a part of it. Suddenly, he felt he had to go back and view the body to be sure he hadn't invented the whole thing. He hoped it had been a bad dream and soon Alvin and Lynda would be walking down the street, arm in arm. Colton snapped the leash on Buck and together they walked to the scene on the crime.

When the dog saw the body, he ran over to it and sniffed it from head to toe. Colton let out a scream of horror and, putting his head between his legs, he began to sob. What kind of monster had he become?

Buck began howling loudly and at the same time, two men with hunting rifles came upon the scene. "My God!" one cried, looking at the dead girl.

The other man ran over to Colton and shook him roughly. "What happened here?" he demanded.

"I don't know. I was walking my dog and found her body. She's my buddy's girlfriend!" he said between sobs.

The man put his arm around Colton's shoulder. "There, there," he said. "Why don't I walk you and your dog home? You need some help right now." He turned to the other man who was standing immobile, staring at Lynda's body. "Don, wake up and get moving! Call the police from your cell phone. I'm going to walk this boy and his dog home."

It was dark when they arrived at Colton's house. The hunter knocked loudly on the door and it was soon answered by Colton's father. "What..." he started to ask when Colton passed out in a dead faint.

"We'd better get him into the house," the man said. "He's had an awful shock."

Together they managed to get the unconscious boy into the living room and placed him on the sofa.

"You'd better sit down," the man told Drew. "I have a harrowing story to tell you."

Hearing the commotion, Katy came running into the room. She took in the scene and clasped her hand over her mouth, shocked to see her son out cold.

"Call Dr. Roberts and tell him to come over," Drew ordered. "Colton's going to need a sedative."

Still not understanding what happened, Katy left the room to do as she was told. She called Buck to follow, but he wouldn't leave Colton's side.

Colton was awake, but he didn't open his eyes. He felt like he never wanted to open them again. He wasn't sure he could face what he had done and the lives he had destroyed.

When the doctor arrived and gave him a shot, Colton pretended to stir and then awaken. Katy ran to his side and hugged him, tears running down her face.

Drew gently pulled her away from her son. "Let him be. Now that he's had the shot, he'll sleep for several hours."

After Colton was helped to bed, he couldn't help but smile. The sedative had dissipated his fear and he was deliriously happy things had worked out the way they had. No one could tie him to the murder now! As he let sleep overtake him, he felt secure in the knowledge he had committed the perfect crime.

## Chapter 10

In the morning, Colton took a long, hot shower, scrubbing himself raw, trying to remove the smell of Lynda from his body. The more he scrubbed, the stronger the scent became. He finally decided to turn the water off and got dressed. He didn't think he would ever rid himself of her scent because he knew his conscience was causing it.

When he went downstairs, Luke Layton, the police chief, was sitting at the kitchen table having coffee with his parents. "Here's my son now," Katy purred.

Luke stood up. "We have to talk, Colton," he said firmly.

"He hasn't had his breakfast yet," his mother objected.

"Button it up, Katy," Drew commanded. "He can eat later." He followed the chief and Colton into the living room.

Katy was hurt that she wasn't asked to join them, but she decided she didn't want to know the details. She cleaned the kitchen from top to bottom, even though she had just done it a few days before. She made all the noise she could to drown out the voices coming from the living room.

Colton sat on the sofa with his head hanging down, the picture of defeat.

"Explain to me exactly what you saw when you and Buck arrived at the scene," Luke said.

"Is this absolutely necessary?" Drew asked.

"Yes it is," the police chief replied with a hint of impatience in his voice. "Would you rather I took him down to the station?"

"No!" Drew exclaimed. "I'm sorry for interrupting, go ahead, Colton."

Colton related the scene exactly as he saw it, stumbling over his words as his eyes darted left and right. "That's all I know," he said softly when he was done.

Just then, there was a loud pounding on the door. "Where is he? I have to talk to him!" Alvin shouted.

Drew recognized Alvin's voice and stated, "It's Colton's best friend and Lynda's boyfriend."

"Good, tell him to come in. I want to speak to him too."

Drew left the room and came back with Alvin in tow. He nervously sat down and glared at Colton. "You were the last one to see her, weren't you?" he exclaimed.

"I left your house before she did. I came here to get Buck and took him out for his evening walk," Colton retorted.

"So you say."

"What the hell is the matter with you?" Colton hollered. "You were there. If you were so worried, why didn't you walk her home?"

The police chief watched the exchange with interest.

"Because obviously you did!" Alvin shouted.

"Are you crazy? I always walk Buck around that time!"

"I know," Alvin said softly. "I'm so upset; I'm taking it out on you."

The police chief rose. "Settle down, fellows," he said. "Emotions are running rampant right now. I think I have everything I need, if not, I know where to find you."

Drew walked him to the door. When he got back, the boys were hugging each other and crying. Drew sat down heavily on a chair. "Katy!" he bellowed. "I need a brandy and make it fast!" He definitely wasn't going to work that day.

## Chapter 11

Colton stayed home for three weeks, refusing to attend school. In the meantime, he had missed two football games.

Coach Gill thought he needed motivation, so he called the Colby house and asked Katy if he could stop by to see him.

"Please do," Katy told him. "Frankly, I don't know what to do with him. He flatly refuses to go to school."

The doorbell rang and Colton answered it. When he saw the coach standing there, he forced a lop-sided grin.

"Hey, tiger," Larry said, playfully punching him on the arm.

Colton stepped back and asked bluntly, "What do you want?"

The coach walked past him into the living room and sat down in a chair. "I came to ask you to come back to school. The students miss you and our team has lost games without you."

Colton shrugged his shoulders. "Your team has lost before," he said coldly.

"Look, Colton, everyone knows the trauma you've been through, but it's time you got back into the swing of things. Lynda's family has finally decided to have her memorial service next weekend and I think you should be there."

"No!" Colton shouted.

Coach Gill went on like he didn't hear him. "The eighth grade class has taken up a collection for a plaque to be placed in the school's newspaper office in her honor. I took the liberty of donating five dollars in your name. With the money left over, we're sending flowers to the service."

"All of that won't bring her back!" Colton howled.

"Of course it won't, stop acting like a baby. Alvin was hurt the most and he'll be there."

"I said I'm not going!" Colton screamed and ran from the room.

Katy walked into the living room. "I take it that it didn't go well."

The coach shook his head sadly. "No, it didn't. I'm at a loss as to what to do with him."

"Drew and I have done everything we can think of, we even made an appointment with a psychiatrist. Of course, Colton says he won't go, but we'll take him kicking and screaming if we have to."

"It sounds like you have a plan. Please keep in touch. I have to go, but I'll talk to you later."

"Thanks for trying to help."

"My pleasure," Larry said and left the Colby house.

## Chapter 12

The day was bright and sunny when Drew drove Colton to his appointment. He decided he would not go into the doctor's office with Colton. He thought he would speak more freely without him there.

About forty-five minutes later, Colton reappeared looking scared and harassed.

"What's wrong?" Drew asked him.

"I think the doctor hypnotized me!"

"So what? You don't have anything to hide."

"I don't remember what I said!" Colton cried.

"Relax, Cutter, you don't come back until next week. By that time, you'll forget about it."

"No I won't," Colton said under his breath.

A week later, a partially decomposed girl was found floating in the quarry by two hikers. The body was unrecognizable, but it was identified through dental records as Morgan Miller.

The county coroner found that drowning was not the cause of death. The girl was hit on the head with a hard object.

Finally, the question of where Morgan Miller had been was answered.

The murder made the headlines in the newspaper, but Colton was confident that it couldn't be linked to him.

The police chief held a meeting with his officers. "We have two unsolved murders in our area. I want to brainstorm to see if we can come up with any ideas."

An officer raised his hand. "Whoever committed the murders lives right here in this town. It's just a matter of time before he strikes again."

"That's a good point," the chief said.

Another officer raised his hand. "I think we should see if the girls had anything in common. Maybe the perp knew both of the victims."

"Good thinking. Is there anything else?"

Officer Gross spoke up. "I think we should check around the state and see if there are any other unsolved crimes that fit the MO."

"The girls were killed in two different manners. Besides, one girl was sexually assaulted and the other one wasn't," the chief pointed out.

A murmur spread over the group.

"Let's get a profiler," someone suggested. "Maybe he could give us some insight as to what kind of person we're looking for."

"The second one could be a copycat killer," another officer volunteered. "The media didn't report how the first girl was killed."

"Okay, boys, we have a start. Clancy, you try and find out what the two girls might have had in common. Bart, you check with the state to see if they have any unsolved murders and I'll contract a profiler. In the meantime, keep your eyes open and your ears peeled for information. I'll expect a report from you next week at the latest."

The chief left the room and the men began talking to each other. No one had any experience in a murder case. Nothing like this had ever happened in Westfield before.

## Chapter 13

After his second appointment with the doctor, Colton came into the waiting room white as a sheet. "Now what's wrong?" his father asked him.

"He made me lay down on the couch and asked me personal things.

"Like what?"

"He asked about my sex life, for God's sake!"

"Son, every boy about your age in experimenting with sex, it's natural."

Colton was ready to object when Drew cut him off. "I know you stole one of my condoms from the nightstand drawer."

Colton's mouth fell open. "That was because I might need one sometime," he said vaguely.

"That's okay, Cutter, it's better to be safe than sorry," his father assured him.

When the two of them got home, Colton went straight to his room. He said he wasn't hungry and refused to come down to eat.

"What's wrong with Cutter?" Katy asked.

"He's upset because the doctor asked him some personal questions," Drew answered without elaborating.

Colton pouted all the way to his next doctor's appointment and Drew had to almost drag him out of the car.

About fifteen minutes into the session, Drew heard loud voices coming from behind the closed door, then Colton came running out. "Go to hell, you quack!" he yelled over his shoulder.

Drew jumped up from his seat and grabbed the boy by the arm, propelling him out the door. The treatment was obviously going nowhere and it was costing him a fortune. They would just have to find another way to help Colton.

Katy went to Children's Services to talk to a counselor. When she arrived, she waited an hour to see Dr. Jane Parker. The woman stood up and said pleasantly, "Hello, Mrs. Colby. Please take a seat."

Katy sat down and looked at the woman expectantly.

"Tell me why you've come to see me."

"My son is a very disturbed boy. He's gone from being a football hero to a total recluse. He won't go to school or associate with any of his friends." Katy felt her eyes mist and she groped in her purse for a tissue.

"What happened to change him?"

"He found a murdered girl when he was walking his dog," Katy said softly. Tears were streaming down her face.

"Can I get you a drink of water or a cup of coffee?"

"I'd love some coffee; I seem to need a boost right now." When she got her coffee, she took a sip and felt measurably better.

"Go on," Jane prodded her.

"He's never been the same since the incident. We tried to take him to a psychiatrist, but the doctor freaked him out and he refused to go back. My husband and I both felt it would be foolish to make him go when it obviously wasn't doing him any good."

"How old is your son?"

"Fourteen going on thirty."

Dr. Parker laughed. "That's a very vulnerable age," she commented. "I can see why he was traumatized."

"It's as if I don't know my son anymore."

"How can we help?" Jane asked kindly.

Katy shrugged. "I really don't know. I was hoping you would have some ideas."

The counselor considered and then opened a drawer and drew out a brochure. She handed it to Katy.

"What's this?" Katy asked.

"It's a ranch up in Lancaster that's for disturbed boys and girls. They rehabilitate them and then return them to their families."

"How much does it cost?" Katy asked, afraid of the answer.

"Oh, don't worry about that, its state funded and won't cost you a dime."

Relieved, Katy asked, "Are there any openings now?"

"I can check, but I'm sure there is. The ranch has a ninety-nine percent success rate," she said proudly.

"I think it's worth a try," Katy said. "I'll take the brochure home and discuss it with my husband. I'll call you in a couple of days." She stood up and gave Jane a heartfelt thank you.

Katy was elated on the way home. She just knew Colton would like it there and would come back as good as new.

She was preparing dinner when Drew came home. "Sit down," she said. "I have something to show you!"

He was taken aback, but waited patiently until Katy returned, clutching the brochure.

"I think I found the solution to Cutter's problems. Read it and see what you think."

Drew looked it over and smiled broadly. "I agree. I want the old Cutter back."

"Alright, I'll call Dr. Parker tomorrow, but you'll have to break the news to Colton."

"Fair enough, I'll talk to him right now." He left the room and Katy could hear his footsteps ascending the stairs.

She waited for an explosion, but none came.  When Drew came back down, she lifted her eyebrows in question.

"Would you believe it?  Colton agreed to go!" he exclaimed.  "He said he wanted to get away from this town and everyone in it."

"Thank God," Katy said, hoping the nightmare would be over soon.

## Chapter 14

Colton liked the ranch at first sight. All the buildings were painted a terra cotta color and were surrounded by pine trees. There was a manmade lake where the residents could swim.

The guide took Carlton to a bunkhouse where there were twenty cots and a metal closet for each one. He showed Colton his bed and told him that lights out was at ten o'clock and revelry was at eight. Breakfast was served promptly at eight thirty, lunch at noon, and dinner at five.

"I'll leave you to get settled in now," the guide said. "When the rest of the guys come in from doing chores, you can get acquainted. Don't forget, dinner's served at five."

Colton unpacked his things and made up his bed as best he could. At home, his mother took care of that.

He lay down on the bed to relax before dinner and fell asleep. He woke up when someone pulled his arm.

"Wake up," a gravelly voice demanded.

Colton sat up in bed and stared at the boy. He looked vaguely familiar. "Who are you?" he asked.

"You don't remember me? No, you wouldn't. You're a super jock and I'm a nobody."

Colton wracked his brain, but still couldn't place him.

"I'm Herb Bauer, a friend of Alvin's."

"Why are you here?" Colton asked.

"Because I'm a klepto. I can't stop stealing. The doctor thinks I'm twisted, so bingo, here I am. The better question is what are you doing here?"

"You probably heard I found Lynda Brown's body. I've never been the same since."

Herb laughed. "I always thought you offed her, then pretended to find her body."

"In your dreams," Colton declared.

"Tell it any way you want. The law bought the story, but it doesn't mean I have to."

Colton turned his back and started straightening his bed.

"See you around, Cutter," Herb said and walked away.

*Great,* Colton thought, *now I have someone watching every move I make.*

Colton went into the mess hall and selected a seat at the end of one of the banquet tables. Soon, all of the seats were full and everyone introduced themselves to Colton. He knew he wouldn't remember all of their names, but at least their faces would be familiar.

A dinner of fried chicken, mashed potatoes and green beans was served family style. Colton was surprised at how good the food was.

The servers were girls who lived at the facility. The girl serving Colton's table was a petite blonde with a simple braid hanging to her waist. Just looking at her made Colton salivate. A stirring in his groin made him afraid the nightmare was starting again.

The girl was clearing plates when Colton approached her. "Hi," he said. "What's your name?"

She winked at him and asked, "Who wants to know?"

Colton blushed and said, "I'm Colton."

"My name's Coleen Nobles," she replied. She looked Colton over and noticed his broad shoulders and narrow waist. His hair was dark and curly and he possessed the most beautiful green eyes she had ever seen.

Colton was evaluating her too. Large breast, full red lips and beautiful blue eyes.

A current passed between them so forceful that Colton wished he could take her in his arms and hold her.

"Now that we've been properly introduced, why don't you meet me at the lake at ten thirty?"

"Isn't that after lights out?"

Coleen laughed. "Of course it is! That's what makes it fun!"

His heart hammering, Colton relented. "It's a deal," he agreed. "I'll see you at ten thirty."

Coleen blew him a kiss and went back to work.

All of the other residents were sleeping when Colton climbed out the window in the restroom. It was a tight squeeze, but he made it. He took care to leave the window open so he could crawl back in.

He ran down to the lake where Coleen was waiting for him. She had taken her hair down and it fell loosely below her waist. In the moonlight she looked like a beautiful creature from another planet. She wore a gauzy nightgown.

When she saw Colton, she ran to him and threw her arms around his neck, pressing her body into his.

Colton lifted her head and kissed her, tasting her full lips.

Boldly, she tangled her tongue with his and he became aroused. Coleen gave out a low, sexy laugh that ended with a moan.

Colton had never felt this way before. Self-conscious, he pulled away from her and took her hand. "Come on, let's sit on the bench and talk."

She obediently followed him and sat so close to him, a thread couldn't have passed between them.

"Why are you here?" Colton asked.

"I worked part time at a jewelry store and the owner caught me stealing, but only after I had already taken fifteen hundred dollars. He didn't prosecute because I'm a minor. Besides, my parents were killed in a car accident a short time earlier."

"I'm sorry," Colton said quietly.

"Don't be. Now I can spread my wings and do anything I want to."

"How old are you?"

"Seventeen," Coleen replied. "I'm small for my age; most people think I'm younger than I am."

*Oh my God,* Colton thought. *She's three years older than me.*

"You play football, don't you? I can tell by your physique."

"Yes, I do. Linebacker for Westfield's varsity," he lied.

Coleen clapped her hands. "I knew it!" she exclaimed.

Just then a flashlight shone on a path about twenty feet from them.

"Come on!" Coleen exclaimed and hid herself in the bushes behind the bench.

Colton followed her and ducked behind the bush just as the man walked by.

"He's the night guard," Coleen explained when he left. "He patrols every half hour. Security's tight around here."

"Oh," was all Colton could say.

Coleen freed herself from the bushes. She took his hand and pulled him out after her. "It's getting late, I have to go. See you tomorrow, same place, same time," she said before running away toward the girl's quarters.

Colton stood and watched her go. He was already looking forward to the next night.

When he got back to the bunkhouse, he was horrified to find the window shut. Frantic, Colton didn't know what to do. He ran all around the quarters, but all of the windows were shut tight. Since he couldn't get in, he decided he would go back to the bench.

He sat down and enjoyed the night's sounds. He was about to nod off when the guard's light flashed over him. "Who's that?" a gruff voice asked.

"Oh, it's just me. I couldn't sleep, so I thought I'd take a walk. It's my first night here."

The man walked over to the bench and put his hand on Colton's shoulder. "It's different being in a strange place, isn't it? You're used to being at home and in your own bed."

Colton nodded his head.

"Come with me, I'll walk you home. The doors lock automatically when you leave. I have keys, so I can let you in."

"Thank you!" Colton exclaimed.

"It's okay, I was a boy once too," he said.

## Chapter 15

Colton saw Coleen every night for three weeks before she shocked him by announcing she was going home in two days. Shaken, Colton knew he couldn't let her go. "What about me?" he asked. "Will I ever see you again?"

"I doubt it," she said coldly. "It was fun when it lasted, but I have to go home now and get on with my life."

Colton was outraged. How could she leave him after all the intimate moments they shared? A coldness washed over him. When she told him she thought she was pregnant, he snapped. *I have to get rid of her,* he thought.

"Honey, I'm so happy for you," he said. "Before you go, I want to show you my home town."

"How could we possibly do that?" she asked.

"We'll just hitch a ride and no one will know we're gone."

"I don't think so."

"Come on, I want to give you something special to remember me by."

"Okay, how would we do it?"

"I'll walk over while everyone's at breakfast and we'll go out to the highway and catch a car going our way."

"I don't care if I get caught now. I'm outta here anyway. Okay, you're on."

It was nine o'clock when they reached the highway. Colton had Coleen stick her thumb out since she was pretty and more likely to get picked up.

A few cars passed without giving them a glance, but an eighteen wheeler ground to a stop.

Colton and Coleen hurried over to the rig. When they opened the door, the burly driver asked them where they were headed.

"Westfield," Colton told him.

"It's right on my way," the driver said. "Jump in."

The drive only took about an hour. "You can pull over any time," Colton said. "We can walk from here."

"Whatever you say." He applied the brakes and pulled over to the shoulder. "Have a good day," he said.

"You too," Colton answered. "Come on, Coleen, we'll take a shortcut to my house."

"I can't wait to meet your folks," Coleen said.

"They'll love you," he answered. He took her by the hand and led her into the woods next to the highway.

"It looks dark in there!" Coleen exclaimed, stopping in her tracks.

"Don't be silly, honey. We'll be there in a flash."

Reluctantly, she followed him. They had only walked a mile when Coleen complained that she was tired.

"It's not far, but we can rest for a minute," Colton said. Coleen sat on a log.

"I have to take a wiz," Colton said, going around the log she was sitting on. He tackled her from behind and knocked her to the ground.

"What are you doing?" she asked, her voice shaking with alarm.

"A little rough sex is good sometimes," he said, pretending to unzip his pants. Instead, he lunged at her, pinning her to the ground. He sat on top of her to hold her down and bent over to give her a soft, lingering kiss.

Coleen's eyes were wide with fear. "What are you doing?" she screamed. "Get off me! This isn't funny!"

"Afraid I'm hurting that little thing in your tummy?" Colton sneered.

"Just get off me!" Large tears ran down her cheeks.

Colton backhanded her across the face, leaving a large, blood red welt.

Coleen struggled to get out from under him, but he was too heavy for her. She finally realized what was happening. "Kill me, I don't care, but you'll pay for it," she whispered. "Go ahead, get it over with."

"First I'm going to play with you, baby. I'm in no rush." Colton broke off a large branch from a pine tree near them.

Coleen lay on the ground, shaking. She covered her eyes, not wanting to see what he was going to do next.

Colton shoved her dress up roughly and ripped her panties off. Taking the large branch, he quickly shoved it into her.

She screamed and blood gushed out of her. There was so much blood that Colton felt with satisfaction that she would be dead within a few minutes. "Sorry, baby," he crooned as he picked her up and dumped her body in a deep ditch on the side of the road.

He looked down at her and laughed. "Thought you'd catch me with that pregnancy stuff, did you? I forgot to tell you I'm only fourteen years old."

Colton looked himself over to be sure he didn't have any blood on him, then calmly walked across the road to hitch a ride back to the ranch.

He made sure he got there right after a bus had pulled into the Lancaster terminal.

Colton was strolling back to the bunkhouse when the headmaster stopped him. "How's your mother?" he asked.

"She's much better, thank you, but I'm glad I went home to see her."

"When you got the letter saying you had to come home at once, I thought your mother was on her death bed."

"She surprised everyone when she rallied. I'm tired now, so I'm going to lie down on my cot and rest."

"Go along, son. I'm glad everything turned out alright for you."

Colton turned away to hide his smile.

## Chapter 16

The police chief called another meeting. "Okay, gentlemen, it's been a week. What have we got?"

The group moaned, but one lone officer raised his hand. "I went back to the scene of the crime and searched the area." He reached in his pocket and pulled out a swiss army knife. "I found this about four feet from where the victim was murdered. It was buried in the mud."

"Let me see it," the chief commanded. He turned the knife over in his hand. "This may or may not belong to the murderer. These things are a dime a dozen and can be purchased anywhere. Stan, get me an evidence bag and we'll keep it until we have more to go on. Anyone have anything else to report?"

Everyone shook their head no.

"Okay, fellows, what do we have? There were two boys that knew Lynda well, Alvin Arneson and Colton Colby. I say we question both of them again."

An officer came running in the door. "I think you should get out here immediately. An elderly couple on vacation were riding down the highway and saw a body in a ditch."

Luke ran out the door and saw an old man and woman clinging together. The woman was crying.

"Please come into my office," the chief said, showing them the way.

They sat down stiffly, both of them afraid.

"Did you call 911 when you discovered the body?"

The man shook his head no. "We were so scared; we got out of there as fast as we could. We drove straight here."

"You mean the body is still lying there?"

The couple both nodded.

"Jesus Christ!" he yelled. "Jan, get me the coroner on the phone right now!"

When he was on the line, the chief picked up the phone and said. "Digger, get over to the station and pick me up. There's been another murder. I'll call an ambulance to meet us there."

He ran back into the room where the meeting was held. The men were still there, talking amongst themselves. "We've got another one!" the chief shouted. "I'm on my way out there now. I'll keep you posted."

When the coroner arrived, the chief jumped in his van and they took off with tires squealing.

"Where exactly are we headed?"

"As near as I can figure, about six miles north of the city."

"North?"

"North," the chief replied.

The coroner made a u-turn and sped in the other direction.

"I'm not sure of the exact location; we'll have to keep a sharp eye out." The chief filled Digger in on the conversation with the old couple.

"You mean they just took off and left her there, not knowing if she was dead or alive?"

"I'm afraid so. At least they had enough sense to come directly to the station."

"Where are they now?"

"I have an officer taking their statements. After that, he's going to check them into a motel. We'd like to have them stick around for a while."

The coroner pointed up the road. "I'll bet that's the place we're looking for. She's already drawn a crowd."

A maroon Cadillac was pulled over on the shoulder of the road with a green Chevrolet parked behind it. Six people were staring down into the ditch.

The coroner's van screeched to a halt and the chief jumped out. "Move along, folks, this is a crime scene.

Don't make it a circus." When no one moved, the chief took out his gun. "I'm Luke Layton, the chief of police in this jurisdiction. Now I said move it!"

This time the bystanders jumped in their cars and left in a hurry. They had just gone when the ambulance drove up, lights flashing. Quickly, they got a gurney out of the back and wheeled it toward the ditch.

"Hold on," the coroner said. "I haven't had time to check out the body yet."

The two EMS workers walked back to their vehicle and lit up cigarettes.

The chief was repulsed by what he saw in the ditch. A girl lay in a mass of blood, a fetus by her side. He had seen many dead people, but this was the worst. He had to put his hand over his mouth to keep the bile down.

The coroner took one look and motioned the EMTs over. "Take her to the morgue. I'll examine her there."

The men loaded the body on the gurney and put the fetus in a black plastic bag. Luke and Digger got into the van and followed the ambulance. "You coming along?" the coroner asked.

"I've got things I have to take care of at the station," the chief lied. "Call me when you're finished and we'll make out a detailed report together."

Later that day, the coroner came to Luke's office to talk things over. "Tell me the story," the chief said.

"It isn't pretty. Jane Doe was a girl between the ages of fifteen to eighteen years old. Examination of the fetus showed that she was three months pregnant. Her death, and this is the worst part, was caused by someone who drove an object into her vagina so hard that she lost the baby and bled to death."

The chief was horrified. "Was she alive when it happened?"

"I'm afraid so. She probably blacked out after losing all that blood, but it would have taken about an hour."

"Whoever did this is a monster!"

Digger nodded his head, agreeing with the chief.

Luke slammed his fist down on the desk and shouted, "I'm going to nail this beast if it's the last thing I do."

"Settle down, nothing will bring the girl back."

"So many young lives have been viciously snuffed out. I never thought anything like this would happen in Westfield. The residents are scared and almost everyone I know has bought a gun. Most of them don't know how to shoot and will probably end up shooting an innocent person. No one will let their daughters out alone after dark. The most important thing is that no one should trust anyone until this is over."

"We can give that thought across when we give the story to the Gazette." The coroner got up to leave. "I'd buy you a cup of coffee, Luke, if I wasn't so damn tired. All I want to do is go home and get some shuteye."

Luke patted the coroner on the back. "Have a good sleep if you can, my friend. Tomorrow's another day."

"I can't wait," Digger said sarcastically.

With the help of the coroner's report, Luke wrote an article for the Gazette the next day. He tried to state the facts, but left out the cause of death. People were crazed already and he didn't want to add fuel to the fire.

After he dropped the article off at the paper, he went to a meeting he had scheduled with his officers. The profiler was supposed to speak.

## Chapter 17

The profiler got up in front of the group and consulted his notes. "Our suspect is a disturbed young man, probably between the ages of eighteen and twenty-five. He most likely comes from a good family, possibly an only child used to getting his way. No doubt he's clean cut and does everything in his power to conceal the beast he is. He's also cunning, gaining the trust of his victims before he makes his move. There's no doubt he knew all of them well. A person of this nature usually has a doting mother who he hates for smothering him. Every time he kills, he thinks he's killing her. He could be homosexual, but I doubt it. I feel he's a large, strong man that can easily overpower a woman."

He stopped talking and looked at the chief. "All of this is just my opinion, but in all of the work I've done in this field, I've been right ninety-five percent of the time."

The chief thanked him and he took his leave to move on to another unsolved case.

After he left, the chief said, "There it is, guys. Now get out there and find our man. We've got to catch him before he kills again."

The chief decided to advise the media of the profiler's description in hope that the tactic would scare the perp into thinking the police were on to him. If he panicked, maybe he would make a mistake.

A foolish thought invaded Luke's brain and he almost cast it aside. He reconsidered and picked up the phone to call an old friend.

"Brookside Police Department," a man answered.

"Hello, is Chief Major in?"

"Yes sir, I'll put you through."

A hearty voice came on the line. "Mark speaking."

"Hey, you old devil. How are you?"

There was a pause and then the man replied, "Luke? Is that you?"

"Yeah, long time no see."

"You can say that again! Sometimes I think of the Watson case we cracked together. What can I do for you?"

"I read somewhere that you used a psychic to help you close a case. I'd like you to tell me more about her."

Mark chuckled. "Phyllis Ralston is a character, but she's good at what she does."

"Could you give me her phone number so I can call her? God knows I could use some help."

"Alright, I've got her number in my rolodex. Hang on a minute." He came back on the line and recited a series of numbers. "I must warn you, Luke, Phyllis is an eccentric who won't work with many people."

"You know me; I'm a silver tongued devil."

Mark laughed. "Good luck," he said. "I'm going to collect on that beer you owe me one of these days."

"Let's make a date or we'll never get around to it."

"I'll call you soon," he answered.

The chief called Phyllis Ralston immediately.

"Hi, it's me," a cheerful voice answered.

Luke decided to follow suit. "Hi yourself, it's me, Chief Layton of the Westfield Police Department."

"What do you want, sweetie?"

"Mark Major said I should give you a call. My department is badly in need of your help."

"I don't work for just anyone."

"I'm somebody, all sugar and spice and everything nice."

"How boring! What kind of a police chief are you?"

Luke tried again. "I'm a big, mean officer who chases women."

Phyllis laughed. "That's more like it," she said. "Your place or mine?"

Luke wondered what Mark had gotten him into. He said soberly, "We're hunting a killer who has already murdered three young girls. I really need your help."

Phyllis chuckled. "I was just putting you on. Anyone Mark recommends, I'll work with anytime."

Luke breathed a sigh of relief. "I'll send you a ticket to fly up to Westfield."

"I'll be there with bells on as soon as I receive it."

"I'll overnight it. I need you yesterday."

## Chapter 18

The phone buzzed in the chief's office two days later. The receptionist said soberly, "A Ms. Ralston to see you," and then started laughing.

"Send her in." The chief made a mental note to chastise the girl later.

After a bit, the door opened and Luke almost fell off his chair. He stared at a large boned woman with an orange afro. She wore a miniskirt three inches above her knees and her sunglasses had large plastic frames tilted up at the corners with rhinestones sparkling all over them. The chief cleared his throat and got a hold of himself. He stood and offered his hand. "Phyllis, it's a pleasure. Please sit down and we'll talk."

When she sat down, her skirt inched to her thigh, exposing more than the chief wanted to see.

"Let's get down to business," he said.

"Let's do," she said. "First I want you to take me to the scene of each crime and we'll go from there. I don't guarantee results, but I'm usually on target."

"We'll do that first thing in the morning. I've reserved a room for you at the Westfield Motel, where I think you'll be comfortable, but..."

The woman laughed. "My clothes? I only dress this way to shock people, even my hair is phony." She pulled on a lock of hair and the wig fell down over her forehead.

Luke breathed a sigh of relief.

The chief picked Phyllis up at nine o'clock the next morning. He didn't recognize her as the same woman. She had on a tailored tweed suit and her greying hair was pinned into a bun at the base of her neck. She had on brown flats and no makeup except for a touch of lipstick.

"This is the real Phyllis, at your service," she quipped.

"I'm pleased and relieved to meet you."

"Where are we going?"

"To a wooded area down the road a piece.  The ride will only take about fifteen minutes."


Colton was happy to get back to the ranch and the familiar routine.  Several days later, he was eating breakfast when he heard two of the waitresses speculating about Coleen's disappearance.

"I think she ran away with Jake," one girl said.  "She was seeing him again."

"It wouldn't surprise me if he did her in," another girl said.  "He has a violent temper."

The girls walked into the kitchen where Colton couldn't hear the rest of their conversation.  He got up from the table elated, the blame had fallen on someone else.  He knew he was very lucky and vowed that he would never do such a horrible thing to anyone again.

Colton actually whistled as he walked back to the bunkhouse to clean the restroom, the job he had been assigned.

## Chapter 19

The chief led Phyllis to the woods surrounding the ditch where Coleen's body was found.

She motioned him away and her eyes took on a faraway look. She held her hands and walked in larger and larger circles, examining the ground. Phyllis stopped in a clearing where the sand had a deep indentation that could have been caused by someone dragging a body. She covered her ears with her hands and let out a loud, piercing scream.

Luke rushed to her side. "What's wrong?" he asked, alarmed.

Phyllis waved him away. "I feel him here, his presence is very strong," she whispered.

She followed an imaginary trail that finally led to the ditch. Phyllis turned and looked at him. "She was killed where we were and dragged to the ditch."

"Do you know who murdered her?"

"No, but the crime was committed in a fit of passion. My feelings tell me that whoever did this was in a rage and out of control."

"Can you tell who it is?"

"No, the picture's too cloudy. I visualize a large man, but I can't make out the features. I have the overwhelming feeling he was on foot. He didn't have any transportation."

Just then, a Greyhound roared by. "That's it!" she said. He left the scene on a bus!"

Luke's mouth fell open. "Are you sure?"

"I'm right as rain," she said. "Take me to the other scenes; I think there's a connection."

The chief was dumbfounded. "That's back the other way, close to town," he said vaguely.

"That's beside the point, Buster," Phyllis said smugly. "You want me to help you apprehend the killer, don't you?"

Luke didn't say a word, just started walking to the squad car. He could hear Phyllis laughing as she followed behind him.

## Chapter 20

Colton couldn't sleep, his demons kept showing their ugly faces. He tossed and turned until he couldn't stand it anymore. He sat up and put his feet on the cold tile floor.

He only had four nights left at the ranch. In a way, he was sorry to leave the security of the place, on the other hand, he was anxious to get home. He missed his parents, his dog, and especially football.

Knowing sleep was out of the question, he decided to use his old escape routine one more time. A vision of Coleen passed through him, but he pushed it aside. After all, the past was the past and he couldn't change it, but he could look forward to a bright future in football.

He snuck through the sleeping bodies and entered the spotless restroom. He wedged himself through the window and dropped to the ground. Colton jogged the trail to the pond and sat down on the bench. Relaxed, he looked up at the stars and listened to the faint movement of water.

Suddenly, a hand clamped on his shoulder and something was thrown in his lap. Colton turned around quickly and there stood Herb Bauer with a gap toothed grin on his face. "Hello, lover boy," he sneered.

Colton was shocked to see the dislike written on his face. "What are you doing here?" he asked.

"Just checking out where you were going now that Coleen's missing."

"What do you mean by that?"

"This isn't the first time I've followed you to this spot."

An alarm sounded in Colton's brain and bile threatened to invade his throat. "What the hell does that mean?" he asked tersely.

"I've followed you many nights to watch your trysts with Coleen."

Colton clenched his fists and wanted to knock Herb out cold. Instead, he tried the comradely approach. "Boys will be boys," he said, forcing a grin.

"But not all boys are killers, are they? Read the newspaper," Herb said, pointing to the Westfield Gazette he had dropped on Colton's lap. He handed Colton a flashlight. "Read it!" he demanded.

The headline read "Murdered Girl Found in Ditch". The article went on to say that the police were not releasing the cause of death. Colton's heart began to race. "What interest could I possibly have in this?" he asked.

"Everyone thinks Coleen left with her boyfriend, but we know better, don't we?"

"What are you talking about?" Colton shouted.

"You snuck out and offed her." He pointed at a paragraph in the article. "It says here the girl was three months pregnant. She tried to blame it on you, but you weren't around three months ago, were you?" Herb said, picking up the paper and waving it under Colton's nose.

He batted it away with his meaty hand. "You son of a bitch, I could squash you like a bug," he threatened.

"Try it and I'll go straight to the police with my story."

"They'll never believe you."

"Are you willing to take that chance?"

Colton considered. What he wanted to do is kill Herb and throw his body in the pond. "You'd just better watch your step," he said.

"Or what?" Herb jeered. "I've got your sorry ass over a barrel, hot shot."

"My parents don't have any money, you know that."

"That's not what I want. I want to bring you down and end your football career forever."

Colton's stomach lurched. "Just how do you plan on doing that?"

"I know a big bruiser that plays for Crandon High. He owes me one. If I ask him, he'll break every bone in your body."

"Ha!" Colton laughed. "I can handle anyone on the football field."

"Not this guy, you can't. He's big and mean and stronger than you."

"Big deal," Colton said, but his gut started to quiver.

"Think about it, pal," Herb snarled. "Watch your back."

Just then a flashlight panned the area, catching the two of them in its beam. "Who's there?" the security guard called.

"It's just Colton and I having a late night chat," Herb answered.

The guard came closer. "This is getting to be a habit with you, isn't it?" he asked Colton.

Colton pasted a big smile on his face. "I only have a few days left. I came out here one last time."

"Okay boys, come with me and I'll let you back in your bunkhouse."

Colton deliberately walked in front with the guard, leaving Herb to follow behind.

Colton thanked the guard and they entered the building. "Don't forget to watch your back, boy," Herb hissed.

## Chapter 21

The chief and Phyllis arrived at the quarry where the officer had found the pocket knife.  As soon as she got there, Phyllis stiffened. "There are very bad vibes here," she said. "There is a definite connection to the other murder. I sense the same rage. The same person killed both girls."

Luke felt overwhelmed and completely worn out. "Let's call it a day," he said. "I've had about all I can take."

"Buck up, buddy," Phyllis answered. "The fun has just begun."

Before leaving the ranch, each person was called into the guidance counselor's office for an evaluation. Colton arrived early to make a good impression. When his name was called, he put on a happy face and entered the counselor's office.

"Hello, sir," he said, walking to the desk and extending his hand. The two shook hands and Colton sat down in the chair facing the desk.

"Well, Colton, are you glad to be going home?"

"Yes, sir," he replied.

The counselor opened a manila folder with Colton's name on it. He leafed through it and closed it, looking at Colton. He smiled. "You've been a model resident here, Colton, except for a few minor incidents. I see you have a penchant for roaming around at night. The guard reported he brought you back to the bunkhouse twice. Your file also says you were exemplary in cleaning the restrooms and never refused to do anything asked of you. Well, that's it, I declare you rehabilitated."

The man stood up and shook Colton's hand again. "Good luck," he said as Colton walked out the door.

Herb Bauer brushed shoulders with him as he entered the counselor's office. He had an ugly expression his face.

*He must be in trouble,* Colton thought. His fist fights with all the residents were legendary.

Colton quickly got his things together and waited for the bus. On the way back to Westfield, he closed his eyes tightly when he passed the place where he had thrown Coleen's body. The closer Colton got to home, the more agitated he became. He was returning to the life he had left behind, a doting mother and a milk toast father. He wished he was going off to college; instead the bus was taking him back to his worst nightmares.

Colton's parents met him at the bus station. He exited the bus with a big smile on his face.

Katy ran to him and gave him a huge hug. "My baby's home!" she cried, squeezing his hand in hers.

Drew stood quietly, viewing the scene. "Good to have you back, Colton," he simply said. He hoped the boy had changed, but he had his doubts.

His thoughts were confirmed when they settled themselves into the station wagon. "When are you going to get rid of this old rat trap?" Colton asked with disgust.

"Now, honey," his mother said. "You know we can't afford a new car."

Colton didn't say another word and Drew ignored the whole exchange.

A large moving van sat in front of the Arneson home. Colton saw Alvin struggling to load a large box into the back of the van while two men carried out the living room sofa. "What's going on?" Colton asked.

"The Arneson's are moving," his father said flatly.

"Why?"

"Henry got transferred to Ohio," his mother replied.

"Oh," Colton said.

Drew stopped the car and the three of them got out. Colton was getting his things out of the trunk when Alvin waved at him. He gave him a short wave back and hurried into the house.

"Wait, son," Katy called. "Don't you want to say goodbye to Alvin?"

"Later," Colton replied. "I want to take my things up to my room first."

His father frowned, but said nothing.

Colton put his things away slowly, then made a fuss over Buck, who was running around in circles, happy to see him.

"The moving van is ready to pull out. You better hurry!" Katy called from downstairs.

"I'll be down in a minute. I'm almost finished," Colton called back. He puttered around until he heard the moving van leave and then bounded down the stairs, pretending to be in a hurry.

"Oh, baby, you just missed him. The van just left."

"I'm sorry," Colton said vaguely. He ran outside with Buck to play in the yard.

Drew looked after them, a deep frown on his face. He knew exactly what Colton had done.

"I'm taking Buck for a walk," Colton announced when he came back in the house.

"Okay, but come back soon, we've missed you," Katy said, twisting his hair in her fingers.

Colton tried to turn his head, but she kept twisting his hair. "So soft," she cooed.

"Later," he said, running to get Buck's leash. The boy and his dog ran out the door and down the steps while Katy watched them go with affection.

Drew came up behind her and gave her a quick squeeze. "Give him some space, honey," he said. "He needs some time to adjust to being back home."

When Colton and Buck approached the quarry, there were two people standing at the exact location where he had killed Morgan. Colton recognized one of them as Chief Layton. He had never seen the woman before.

Buck started to bark, but Colton shushed him and pulled him behind some tall bushes where they couldn't be seen.

The two people were engaged in an animated discussion and the chief was checking the ground, as if looking for clues.

*How could they know that was where I killed Morgan?* Colton wondered. She had been found floating in the quarry.

He realized the hopelessness of staying there any longer. He wasn't close enough to hear what was going on. Besides, Buck was getting restless.

Colton moved out of the bushes and they made their way back down the path.

When the two of them arrived home, Colton dutifully removed his dirty sneakers and placed them outside the door. His mother looked at him with disdain. "I thought you were never coming back! My meal has been in the oven for over two hours, I'm sure it's ruined by now."

Colton looked at her and said sharply, "I'm not hungry, Mom."

Katy looked at him with disbelief. "I made your favorite, chicken and dumplings!"

"Sorry," Colton said coldly. "All I want to do is sleep in my own bed. The cot at the ranch was the pits." He ran up the stairs, wanting to get as far away from his parents as possible.

Katy put her hands on her hips and said, "Well I never."

Drew patted her arm. "Remember, Cutter just returned today. It will take him some time to adjust to living here again. Come on, let's eat before the chicken gets too dried out."

Katy didn't reply. She went in the kitchen and removed one plate from the table. She took the dinner out of the oven and they sat down to eat alone.

## Chapter 22

The chief called another meeting the next day.  He introduced Phyllis, who explained that she could sense a presence both in the woods and at the quarry, but couldn't see the face of the killer.  The only thing she knew was that it was a man.

"Where do we go from here?" someone asked.  "We can't interview Alvin again; his family moved to Ohio and Colton was out of town when the third murder was committed.  That just leaves Greg, and his father's attorney won't let us near him."

"Bullshit," the chief said.  "We'll serve him with a subpoena.  He'll have to appear."

"I'd like to sit in on the meeting," Phyllis said.  "Perhaps I could get some new information for you."

"Are we all in agreement then?" Luke asked.

Everyone nodded their heads.

"Okay, I'll make the subpoena date two days from now at three o'clock in the afternoon.  Everyone get back to work."

That night, Buck kept barking and scratching at the door.  It was unusual for him to want to go out so late, so Colton walked out with him.

The dog ran directly to something lying in the grass.  "Buck, no!" Colton hollered.

The dog reluctantly stopped sniffing whatever it was.

Colton walked over and saw a clump of raw hamburger meat.  He had no doubt it was poisoned.  Colton knew exactly who did it, so he went back into the house and called the chief of police, who promised he'd be right over.

Colton gave Buck a dog biscuit and petted his coarse coat.  He was shaking with anger.  What would he do without his only friend?

When the chief arrived, he said, "Okay, let's see that hamburger that's got you so upset."

"Come outside," Colton said.

The chief examined the meat and put it in an evidence bag. "We'll get this checked out," he promised.

Buck, hearing a strange voice, came running to the men. He started sniffing Luke's shoes.

"He must smell your dog," Colton said.

Buck lifted his leg and peed all over Luke's shoe.

"What the hell?" he roared. "Get that beast away from me!"

Colton was embarrassed, but started laughing and couldn't stop. "Call me when you get the report," he said, holding his stomach.

The chief looked disgusted and left with a brisk, "Later."

Colton vowed he would pay Herb back for trying to kill his dog, but it would take some time to figure it out. He rode his bike past Herb's house several times, but it looked deserted. There was no car, no bike and the lawn hadn't been mowed for weeks. He knew he had to hit Herb where it hurt and end this ridiculous vendetta.

## Chapter 23

Coach Gill called Colton at home one afternoon. He was outside giving Buck a bath, so he didn't hear the phone until it was too late. He checked the caller ID and was happy to see the coach had called. Colton hadn't contacted him because he wasn't sure what kind of reception he'd get.

Quickly, he dialed the number and the coach's familiar voice came on the line. "Hi Coach," he said simply.

"Cutter, is that you? I just tried to call your house."

"I know, that's why I'm returning your call."

"Welcome back! I called to tell you that the varsity team is practicing right now, getting ready for next season. I sure would like you to come aboard. I'm not the head coach of the varsity, but I act as an assistant. Come to practice Saturday morning at ten and I'll introduce you."

Colton's heart leapt with joy. He was going to get to play football again!

Colton knew a lot of the varsity players because he had played with them in middle school. Coach Gill introduced him to the other players. Most of them had been on the team for three years and were seniors.

"Here's the linebacker you'll be working with," the coach said, introducing him to a giant, two hundred pound player.

"Pleased to meet you," Colton said.

The boy looked at him indifferently. "Linebackers come and linebackers go," he said in an unfriendly voice.

"I was a linebacker last year, so I know what to do."

"We'll see, I'll show you the ropes."

Colton looked questioningly at Larry.

"Come on," the coach said. "There are other players I want you to meet."

Aside, he told Colton, "That guy's full of himself. He thinks his shit doesn't stink. Come on, son, we'll get you into battle." He handed Colton a helmet. "Put this on, we're going to war," he said laughing.

For a while, the team tackled dummies, did their exercises, and then got down to serious business.

One of the quarterbacks went back to throw the ball. Colton immediately sensed he was throwing to the tight end. He found a hole in the defensive line, ran through and tackled him. The line coach clapped his hands. "Atta boy," he hollered.

Bruce, the huge linebacker, shouted, "Lucky play." Colton ignored him. He knew he was lighter and faster than him, so he didn't let the guy bother him.

After practice, Colton's new coach took him aside. "I see you're going to be a real asset to our team. Just as Larry said, you have that killer instinct.

*Oh boy, killer instinct?* Colton thought. He had put the killings behind him. He had stashed them so far in the back of his mind that it seemed as though they never happened. The only thing that mattered now was football. He wanted to be a super jock.

## Chapter 24

When Colton walked out on the field for the first game, the crowd went crazy and the cheerleaders jumped up and down. Bruce Early frowned. He was used to having the girls cheer for him. It made things worse when there was only a smattering of applause when his name was announced.

Colton hadn't played in a game for a long time, so he got a slow start. He missed several tackles, causing Bruce to sneer at him. That gave him motivation and he played like his old self. Colton sacked the quarterback and hit the offensive line so hard that the players didn't want to get anywhere near him.

Westfield won the game twenty one to seven. The coach patted Colton on the back and said, "Good job."

The cheerleaders gazed at him with awe.

After Colton had showered, he found a group of girls waiting for him. They had pens and paper and wanted Colton's autograph. He signed his name dutifully and turned to walk away.

As he left, he noticed a lone girl hanging back from the rest of the group. She wasn't a knockout like the others, but she was certainly pretty. Colton waved at her, causing her to blush. She averted her gaze and walked away. He was used to girls fawning over him and he took her attitude as a snub.

A loud horn interrupted his thoughts. He glanced over and saw his mother sitting in the old station wagon, waving frantically. He wanted to ignore her, but she kept honking and waving. Colton walked over. "What are you doing here?" he asked angrily.

"I came to give my hero a ride home," she said.

He stared at her with disgust. "Mom, I'm a big boy now and I intend to walk home."

His mother looked shocked. "Your father and I wanted to celebrate with you," she said.

"Go home. I'll be there when I get there." He righted his backpack and walked away.

Katy watched him go. Her eyes misted as she put the car in gear.

## Chapter 25

Greg waited in the lobby of the police station to be called in for his interview while Chief Layton finished another meeting.

Phyllis gave her report. She said she was sorry, but all she could contribute was that the killer was a muscular young man, possibly a school boy. She announced that she was leaving Westfield the next day because she was needed in another situation. The chief was sad to see her go, but she said if he needed her services later, she would come back.

Luke dismissed his men and called Greg in. He was accompanied by his father and his attorney. "What do you want with my son now?" his father shouted before they even sat down.

"Button up, John," Luke said calmly. Greg's become our number one suspect."

Steve Wheeler stood up and shouted, "On what grounds?"

"Leave the room," Chief Layton ordered. "I want to have a private conversation with Greg."

"Not on your life!" John exploded.

The chief called Officers Wade and Gross into the room. He pointed at John and Steve. "Get them out of here," he said.

The officers took the two men roughly by the arms and hauled them out of the room.

The chief looked at Greg. "Tell me why you shouldn't be considered a suspect."

"I might as well tell you the truth," Greg replied. "Morgan and I were going steady when Colton tried to move in. I was furious and jealous. Her friends goaded her into leading him on, made a bet with her. To make a long story short, Colton found out about it. I think he killed her for revenge."

"Maybe you did because she looked at another guy."

"That's ridiculous, I loved her." Tears welled up in his eyes and he whispered, "I miss her."

The chief reached in his pocket and pulled out the swiss army knife. "Is this yours?" he asked Greg.

"I had one like it, every kid does."

"Had? As in past tense?"

"I lost mine somewhere."

"Could it have been at the scene of the crime? An officer found it there."

"No!" Greg shouted. "I wasn't there!"

"Okay, that's it for now. Don't go anywhere; I'll want to talk to you again."

Greg got up and ran out the door.

Officer Wade came in. "How'd it go?"

"I feel sorry for the boy. I believed him when he said he was innocent."

## Chapter 26

Westfield High won their first three games. Colton had regained his form and was influential in the victories. He bathed in the glory and forgot all about his sordid past.

Colton learned the shy girl's name was Patty and she was a new student. He befriended her and soon they became an item. He was fascinated by her. She was unlike any girl he had known.

One day, he asked her to take a walk with him and she readily agreed. They came to a downed tree and sat down on it. "How did you end up in Westfield?" Colton asked.

"I moved here with my adopted parents," Patty replied. "My dad had a job opportunity here."

"Adopted?"

"Yeah, my parents were killed in a car accident when I was ten. I didn't have any living relatives, so I was put up for adoption."

"I'm so sorry," Colton said.

"Don't be. My adopted parents are wonderful people and have raised me just like I was their own."

"I'm glad they brought you here."

Patty blushed and smiled, displaying deep dimples in her cheeks. "I am too," she said quietly. "What about you?"

"Not much to tell. I've lived here all of my life. My father played football at Westfield and I'm following in his footsteps. Dad's a great guy, but my mother rules the roost. Unfortunately, I'm the apple of her eye."

"Why is that unfortunate?"

"Because she smothers me."

"I wish I had such a small problem in my life."

"What do you mean?"

"I've never told anyone this before, but I want to tell you."

"What is it?  Please tell me."

Patty looked embarrassed.  "My real father molested me since I was four years old."

"That's terrible!  Didn't your mother know about it?"

"Of course she knew about it, but she looked the other way."

"Oh, honey," Colton said, taking her hand in his.  "I want to protect you from any further hurt."

After a while, they walked back to Westfield hand in hand.  Colton felt sad when he had to say good-bye.  For once in his life, he didn't want to harm the girl he was with.

From then on, Colton and Patty were seldom apart and Colton felt that he was falling in love.

## Chapter 27

Colton had not forgotten that he still had to get back at Herb Bauer. He kept checking the house he lived in, but it still looked vacant. Colton came to the conclusion that the house was dark because the electric bill wasn't paid.

On the pretense of being a concerned relative, he asked the neighbors if they had seen Herb.

They all agreed he was no good and caused his mother nothing but problems. They went on to say the woman worked two jobs to make ends meet. Her husband had run out on her shortly after Herb was born.

Colton asked the best time to go see her and was told she cleaned houses during the day and worked as a waitress at night. Her shift was over at nine o'clock and she walked home then.

Colton was delighted. He had an opportunity to hurt her then, although he doubted Herb would care.

He went home and put on his black jeans and a black turtleneck. He had a black stocking cap he could pull down over his face. Colton's parents thought that he was in his bedroom studying, so he crept down the stairs and out the back door. Buck wanted to come with him, but he shut the door in the dog's face.

Colton hid behind a tree until Herb's mother approached. She was very thin and her shoulders were slumped. Her shoes were old and she walked on the sides of them.

He followed her silently for a while, waiting for the right time to jump her. Once, she paused and looked behind her. Colton should have made his move then, but he couldn't do it. The poor woman had enough problems and suddenly he didn't want to hurt her. He turned around and headed for home.

He knew what he could do to hurt Herb. He would fix the brakes on his beat up bike so when he rode down the hill, he would crash. Colton turned around and went back to Herb's house. He snuck behind the house and saw the red bike lying on the ground. It didn't take him long to take out a few screws to make the bike unsafe.

Two days later, the Gazette ran a picture of a boy lying on the street next to a mangled bicycle. The article said it was the fourteenth fatality in Westfield that year. *Well,* Colton thought. *I guess my killing days aren't over yet.* He felt no remorse, in fact, he felt on top of the world. Herb's demise was like a shot in the arm.

## Chapter 28

He rode his bike over to Patty's one night. When Patty told him her parents weren't home, he decided to take advantage of the situation.

After talking for a few minutes, Colton put his arm around her.

Feeling cozy, Patty rested her head on his shoulder.

Gently, Colton rubbed one of her breasts. She didn't move, so he slid his hand under the leg of her shorts and caressed her thigh. He kissed her deeply, his tongue searching beyond her open lips.

When he pressed between her thighs, she slapped his hand away. "Stop, Colton!" she cried. "You know what I've been through! I'll probably never want to have sex again!"

Colton was taken aback, but not deterred. He pushed her down on the sofa and laid his body on top of hers.

"No!" she screamed. "You're suffocating me!"

When Colton lowered his head to kiss her, she bit his lip as hard as she could. Blood spattered all over his shirt and her tank top.

He put his hand to his lip and yelled, "Get me a paper towel!"

Patty, sorry for what she had done, ran out of the room and returned with a washcloth. She handed it to him and he pressed it to his lip.

Neither one of them said a word. Colton wanted to hit her, but stopped himself. Her folks knew he was coming over, so if he hurt her badly, they'd know who was responsible. He had a powerful urge to put his hands around her neck and squeeze the life out of her. He got up abruptly and left the house, slamming the door behind him. Colton could hear Patty sobbing, but he didn't care.

Katy spotted Colton's cut lip at once. "My poor baby," she crooned. "What happened to you?"

Colton snapped. "Shut up! Just shut up for God's sake! You're treating me like a baby!" He wanted to slap her, but pulled himself together. "I'm going upstairs!" he shouted. "I want to get as far away from you as possible!"

Drew was standing in the doorway and heard the whole thing. He stepped forward angrily. "Now you've done it, Katy. I've warned you before to stop fawning over him like a baby. He was bound to rebel sooner or later."

"I only wanted to console him," she cried.

"You sure did a good job of it. If Cutter never talks to you again, I wouldn't blame him."

Katy stared at Drew as he left the room. She didn't think she'd done anything wrong.

It was days before anyone spoke. Drew hoped Katy had finally learned a lesson.

The killer instinct had taken over Colton's mind again. His hands gripped in frustration wondering who he should kill next.

## Chapter 29

Colton took his rage to the football field. He blasted every boy that came near him, causing two of the boys from the opposing team to be carried off the field on stretchers.

With the big gap in the other team's offensive line, Westfield ran right through them, sacking the quarterback. The team won the game by two touchdowns. The fans went wild.

Coach Wilson looked at Colton thoughtfully. He had never in his career told a player to stop hitting so hard, but Colton acted like the devil himself. The coach put it off and didn't think about it until the next time he played.

The game was out of town. The team had a good record. Colton played well, but without his usual killer instinct. The coach breathed a sigh of relief. Maybe he wouldn't have to talk to him after all.

Colton was just playing the waiting game until he decided who his next victim would be. After the game, the opportunity presented itself. "I'm going to run across the street and get a bucket of chicken," he announced.

The team cheered, knowing they would have a good snack to eat on the bus.

Colton started down the alley and one of the cheerleaders from the opposing team ran after him. "Wait up," she shouted.

Colton pretended he didn't hear her and continued walking. He could hear the girl's footsteps running after him. He stopped abruptly and turned around.

The girl was a beautiful red head with a great figure. "What do you want?" he asked.

She ran up and shoved a piece of paper and a pen at him. "I want your autograph. You're the best looking player on Westfield's team and you can really play!"

Colton signed his name and then said, "I have a surprise for you, honey." He grabbed her arm and pushed her against a concrete wall.

Colton bent forward and she wiggled with delight, thinking he was going to kiss her. Instead, he slammed her head into the wall and stared into her green eyes. "You didn't count on my strength," he said.

"No!" she cried, shaking violently.

"A big bruiser like me always gets what he wants," Colton bragged.

Her eyes looked into Colton's in terror and he slammed her body against the wall. He grasped her head and smashed it again and again against the wall. It wasn't much fun for Colton, since she passed out quickly. He gave her head another whack for good measure and she slumped down onto the ground, lying in a heap. Colton picked up the paper with his name scrawled on it and checked her pulse. There was nothing. Smiling, he trotted down the alley and across the street to buy a bucket of chicken.

Several players were standing outside when Colton came running toward them. "What took you so long?" one for them shouted.

He came to a halt in front of them. "It was busy; I had to wait in line."

"The bus is waiting, we better get a move on," one boy said.

The boys ran to the idling bus and climbed up the steps. "Guess what?" one said. "Colton bought us chicken!"

All the boys scrambled to get a piece.

Colton felt elated and satisfied. It wasn't as exciting as Morgan, but it was good enough. The best part is that he had gotten away with murder again.

## Chapter 30

It was late when he got home, but his father was still up watching television. "Did you win?" he asked.

"Yep, by two touchdowns!"

"Good for you!  Sit down, son; I want to talk to you."

It was the last thing Colton wanted to do, but he sat down.

"Aren't you seeing Patty anymore?"

"We had a falling out," Colton replied flatly.

"How come?"

"Well, I..."

"I was your age once and I bet I know what happened."

"What do you think it was?"

"I think your raging hormones got the better of you."

Colton was shocked. "How did you know?"

"I've been there, done that."

"She hates me now.  Patty's the most decent girl I've ever met and I screwed it up."

"Call her tomorrow and apologize.  Invite her over for dinner; I'll make sure your mother cooks something nice."

"You think so?"

"I think she'll relent."

"Okay, I'll give it a try."  Colton wanted to get back in Patty's good graces, so he vowed he wouldn't be a monster again.

He saw Patty in school the next day.  She lowered her eyes and didn't look at him.  Colton put his hand on her arm. "Patty, I'm sorry.  Please forgive me.  I'd like you to come over to my house tonight and have dinner with my family."

Patty brightened. "I'd love to," she said.

"Good, is six o'clock okay?"

"That's fine with me. I'll see you at six."

Colton was pleased. *That was almost too easy,* he thought.

When he got home, he expected to smell good things wafting from the oven. Instead, his father was getting the charcoal out of the shed and the grill was set up in the backyard. "What's going on?"

"Your mother said the weather was great for a cookout and she didn't want to make a big dinner."

"Doesn't she know Patty's coming over?"

"She knows because I told her."

Colton frowned, getting angry.

Seeing the look on his face, Drew said, "I'm sorry, Cutter. I don't know what's wrong with her." But he did know, Katy didn't want to share Colton with anyone. She wanted to be the only female in Colton's life.

"What are we having for dinner?" Colton demanded.

Drew was ashamed of Katy, but he answered the question. "Hot dogs and hamburgers with sweet corn, baked beans and potato salad."

"At least she made potato salad," Drew said, disgusted.

"Actually, she picked up a container at the IGA."

Colton threw his arms up in despair. "We always have steak and baked potatoes when we fire up the grill."

Patty arrived and Colton apologized for the menu. "Colton, I haven't had a cookout for a long time. It doesn't matter what we eat."

*She always knows the right thing to say,* Colton thought.

Just then, Katy came rushing in, obviously winded.

"Where were you?" Cutter asked.

"I had a million chores to do."

"Why couldn't you have done them tomorrow?"

"Because I wanted to do them today," she answered curtly.

"You'd better go get the corn started," Drew said.

"Oh, alright," Katy said, stalking into the house.

"Can I help her?" Patty offered.

"No, you stay here. I'll get the paper plates, napkins and plastic forks. You can put the cloth on the picnic table."

"Good, I need to be of use somehow."

Drew was impressed at how nice Patty was. He thought Colton had made a good choice.

Katy didn't say a word during dinner. Patty was getting nervous and she knocked over her soda. She was horrified. "I'm so sorry!" she cried.

Colton put his hand on her arm. "That's okay, honey. I'll run and get some paper towels."

"Clumsy girl," Katy hissed under her breath.

Colton couldn't wait to get out of there. He whisked Patty through the kitchen and to the front door. Before he could open it, Patty called, "Thank you, Mrs. Colby, it was nice meeting you."

There was no reply.

Colton pulled her through the door. "I'm sorry; I don't know why my mother's in such a foul mood."

"I do," Patty said quietly. "She doesn't like me."

"Nonsense," he said firmly, but he knew it was true.

"God damn it, Katy," Drew said. "You could have at least been civil. It's a good thing I'd never hit a woman, or I'd pop you a good one! Go upstairs; I don't want you in my sight. I'll clean up down here."

Katy stomped up the stairs, but Drew ignored her.

Patty and Colton were about a block from her house when Colton pretended to trip. His foot caught Patty's leg and she fell hard to the ground.

Colton was ready to pounce on her when he stopped abruptly. He didn't want to hurt Patty, he loved her. He couldn't take his anger at his mother out on her.

Colton helped her up and hugged her. "I'm sorry; I stumbled and knocked you down. I'll have to be more careful because I never want to hurt you."

The next day, he went to Wal-Mart and bought Patty a sterling silver friendship ring. He hoped she didn't sense what he started to do the night before, but if she did, he wanted her to forget it.

When he slipped the ring on her finger, he said tenderly, "This will have to do for a few years when I can buy you the real thing."

Patty gave him a sweet smile. "It's beautiful, Colton. I'll never take it off."

He kissed her lightly on her full lips. "You're so sweet," he murmured.

## Chapter 31

Greg's father, John, had been agitated since the last visit to the police station. There was no damn way his son was going to be treated like a criminal. Finally, he thought of an answer. He called Greg into his den and told him to sit down.

As usual, Greg did as his father commanded. He was afraid of him and would be glad when he went to college.

"I'm going to send you to Costa Rica where you'll be out of harm's way," John told his son. "You're under fire here for no reason. It will only be for a few months until everything settles down. You can stay with Walt; he has a son your age."

Greg jumped out of his chair. "What about school? What about football?" he cried.

You have all A's and the football team won't miss you. You sit on the bench most of the time anyway."

Greg pouted. "I won't go!"

"Yes you will."

John's wife, Lil, entered the room. "Please don't badger the boy, John."

"Don't cross me, Lil, you have no say in the matter."

Lil stuck out her chin. "This time, I do." She had made up her mind she was going to stand up to John this time, but she was afraid she wasn't up to it.

"Get out of here!" John hollered. "Greg and I have things to talk about that don't concern you!"

Hating herself, Lil slunk out of the room like a whipped puppy.

"Now, where were we?"

"I don't want to go to Costa Rica," Greg said belligerently.

"You have no choice in the matter.  I'm going to call Walt tomorrow and get your plane ticket."

"If I leave, the chief will think I'm guilty for sure."

"I'll take care of him," John said smugly.

## Chapter 32

Coach Wilson called Colton aside when he arrived at practice. "Tonight we have a big game with Crawford and I want you to look your best on the field. Scouts are going to be here from Michigan College. They're looking for standout football players and I'm sure you're the one they're here to see. I just wanted to give you a heads up."

That night, Colton walked into the locker room with an attitude. He was ready to hit anyone he came into contact with.

When he stepped out onto the field, he saw two unfamiliar men with suits on sitting in the front row of the bleachers. Colton knew they were the scouts. He pretended to warm up. Out of the corner of his eye, he could see the men watching him intently.

The team huddled together and then yelled, "Let's go!"

Crawford's linebackers must have weighed an average of two hundred twenty pounds and looked formidable.

When Colton got into his defensive position, he had to look one of the bruisers in the eye. "We're gonna make you pay," the guy said grinning, showing a space in his gums where two teeth should have been.

When Westfield's quarterback went back to pass, the player rushed right past Colton and sacked him. He fell hard to the ground and when he got up he was limping. Coach Wilson pulled him out of the game immediately.

The second string quarterback came out and his first pass was intercepted. The fans groaned with disapproval.

The linebacker that had made the interception ran the ball forty yards and Crawford was ahead 7-0.

By halftime, the scoreboard read 14-0. The coach chastised Westfield's linebackers. "You've got to stop them," he shouted.

Colton made some spectacular plays in the second half, but the other team's players were just too big and Crawford won 21-0.

The Westfield team left the field, shoulders slumped, aware that they hadn't played well.

In the locker room, the coach looked at Colton. "You blew it," he hissed.

On the way home, Colton was despondent and the old feeling came over him, but there was no one around for him to hurt.

When he got home, Colton let Buck out and went along with him. The new neighbors' cat was perched on their back steps. When it saw Buck, it ran toward him with curiosity. "Go get him," Colton instructed.

The dog immediately chased the cat, caught it, and took it by the neck, shaking it violently. The cat howled loudly, then it was silent. Colton knew Buck had killed it.

The dog ran up to Colton, looking for praise. Colton obliged by patting Buck's head. "Good boy," he told him.

His mother started on him as soon as he walked in the house. She pointed her finger at him. "What is wrong with you? You cost us the game!" she shouted.

Colton was ashamed, so he turned away from her to go up to his room.

Katy grabbed him by the shoulders. "Get back here, I'm not finished yet!"

Colton shook her hands off him and looked at her with pure hatred. "Leave me alone!" he shouted.

Finally, Drew intervened. "Let him be, Katy. He feels bad enough already."

She glared at him, but didn't say another word.

Colton went to his room with Buck at his heels. He had forgotten all about the episode with the neighbor's cat.

## Chapter 33

The next day, Katy was all smiles. "Did you forget you have a birthday in a few days? Sweet sixteen," she said happily. "Just think, my baby is all grown up!"

Colton made a face at her. "The only thing I'm glad about is that I can get my learner's permit, then my regular driver's license."

Drew walked into the room and said, "Colton, I'll make you a deal. You bring your grades up to a B average and play to your potential on the field and I'll buy you a car."

Katy started to object, but Drew gave her a stern look and said, "Don't get involved in this."

She harrumphed and stalked out of the room.

Colton cut football practice early on his birthday. When he got home, he could smell something baking in the oven. His mother said, "I've made your favorite meal and bought you a birthday cake!"

"I'm sorry, Mom, but I won't be home. Patty and I are going to Mel's for a burger and then to a movie."

"We expected you to celebrate with us," she whined.

"Colton's too old to celebrate every birthday with us," Drew intervened. "In a few years, he'll be off to college."

Katy stuck out her lip. "He'd rather go out with that hussy than to spend tonight with us. She isn't good enough for him."

"I disagree, Patty's a very nice girl. You were wrong to treat her so badly. Let him go, he's been tied to your apron strings for long enough."

Colton, sick of the conversation, took Buck outside.

Drew looked at Katy. "You're driving him further and further away from you. Can't you see that?"

Katy shook her head in denial. "No, he's my only son and I'm going to hang onto him as long as possible."

"He's my only son too, you know. I'll be damned if I'm going to let you make him a mama's boy." He grabbed his jacket off the chair. "I need a drink," he said. "I'll see you when I see you, don't wait up."

Katy wasn't worried. She had been married to Drew for twenty-one years and he had never cheated on her or came home drunk. She busied herself wrapping Colton's birthday present. She signed the mushy card 'Love and kisses, Mom and Dad'.

## Chapter 34

Colton rang the doorbell at Patty's house. "Hi Colton, come on in. Happy birthday!" Mrs. Marlin said. She took his hand and led him to the kitchen. "I made you a chocolate swirl cake. Unfortunately, it lists a little, but I'm sure it will taste good. Sit down and I'll get some ice cream out of the freezer."

"Mom, we were going to get cheeseburgers and fries before we went to the movie," Patty said.

"So what? You can eat your dessert first!"

After they finished the cake and ice cream, Patty's father, Joe, said, "You guys better get going or you'll miss your movie. Have a good night."

Patty's mother ran out of the room and came back with a present. "This is Patty's gift for you. She forgot it in all of the excitement."

"You don't have to open it here," Patty said. "You can do it later."

"Bring my daughter home early. It's a school night," Joe reminded Colton.

When they walked away hand in hand, Colton wondered if Patty knew how lucky she was to have such a caring, loving family.

After the movie, Patty and Colton sat on a bench in front of the Rainbow River Bank. The street sign lit up the area like it was daylight. "Aren't you tired of hauling that box around all night?" Patty asked. "Open it up! My grandmother made it!"

Colton ripped open the silver foil paper. The box was large and Patty had taped it on all four sides. "Why did you make it so tough to open?" He took his fingernail and raked it through the tape.

He gazed down at the present. It was a beautiful, white knit sweater with a large red W on the front. Colton squealed with delight. "I love it! All the guys on the team are going to eat their hearts out." He leaned over and kissed her on the cheek. "Thanks, honey, I'll think of you every time I wear it."

When Colton got home, he left the box on the entry table.

"Colton!" his mother called. "Come and open your present, honey."

Colton cringed. He wondered what she had picked up on sale this year. For his last birthday, she had gotten him a pair of men's slippers too large for him. As luck would have it, they fit Drew perfectly, so at least they didn't go to waste.

He walked into the kitchen and Katy handed him a package obviously wrapped in paper salvaged from another present. "Thanks, Mom," he said and opened it.

He looked down at the white sweater in the box. It wasn't coarsely woven like the sweater Patty gave him, it was light weight. Colton gulped and lifted it from the box.

"Mom, it's too small," he said, trying to sound heartbroken.

"No, it can't be, the table it was on said extra-large."

Colton looked at the label and showed it to her. "See? It says it's a medium."

"Oh, no!" Katy wailed.

"You can return it and get the right size."

"No, I can't, all sale items are not returnable."

"I'm sorry," Colton said, but he wasn't. His mother's cheapness was another thing he hated about her. "Where's Dad?" he asked.

"He went out to see some friends,' she lied.

*What friends?* Colton wondered. Katy had made him quit the bowling team and didn't allow him to play poker with the other guys. He pointed a finger at her. "You're lying!" he shouted. "You drove him off. I hope he doesn't come back, he should have left you a long time ago!"

Katy stepped back like she had been slapped. "How can you say such a thing? I clean the house, cook the meals and see that everything is perfect here."

"Get a job! Make some money so you don't have to buy things on sale. Go to the library and find a book on how to cultivate a loving family."

Colton hollered for Buck and they went outside. They made a beeline for a small replica of a log cabin still there from his youth. There was an old blanket and pillow in there. It was cramped, but there was enough room for Colton and Buck to snuggle together. Before he went to sleep, Colton cried a little. "Happy sixteenth birthday," he said to himself. He wished his mother was dead.

## Chapter 35

Greg thought Costa Rica was wonderful. The Hamlin family lived in a subdivision made up of American families and people living on social security. The prices were so reasonable, they were able to live in a three bedroom ranch house and employed a sweet Costa Rican girl who cooked and cleaned for them.

Walt's son, Roland, was a year older than Greg, but the two of them hit it off immediately.

Roland played soccer instead of football and Greg went with him to practice and soon became good enough to play on Roland's team.

On the weekends, the two of them used Roland's wreck of a car to go to the white sand beach. There were many resorts and luxurious condominiums there that were mostly owned by Americans and other foreigners.

The local bar didn't care if the two of them were of age or not and served them all the beer they could drink. Roland and Greg met up with two girls who were educated in the United States. They had attended UCLA, but had returned to their native country.

Greg was a very intelligent boy and could soon speak Spanish fluently.

One day, while the boys were lying on the beach drinking beer, Greg told Roland about the murders that occurred in Westfield.

"There isn't much crime around here, except it's not unusual for someone to sell the same land to two different buyers. That happens a lot," Roland said.

"You're kidding, aren't you? My dad's been talking about buying some land here and moving when he retires."

Roland laughed. "He'd better let my dad handle the transaction for him. He knows the ropes."

"Getting back to the girls' murders, there's a star football player I don't trust. He knew most of the girls that were killed, but the police don't have enough evidence to arrest anyone."

"Who is this guy?"

"The town's hero. Everyone loves him, including the girls. He hit on my girl and, before you knew it, she was dead."

"Have you told the police your beliefs?"

"Yes, but they didn't believe me. I was questioned along with the other guy, but because of his reputation, they let him go. I've been interviewed several times and am their prime suspect. That's why Dad sent me here for a while."

Greg felt more and more at home in Costa Rica and soon became close friends with Rosa, the Hamlin's hired girl. Roland told him she was off limits, but Greg didn't pay any attention to him.

One day, Greg invited Rosa to go to the beach with them. Roland didn't like it, but finally agreed.

Everything was going fine until Rosa drank too much beer in the hot sun. For a while, the boys let her sleep it off on the sand, but dusk was coming soon and Roland had to hurry home before his curfew.

Greg picked the sleeping girl up and carried her to the car. He placed her in the backseat and crawled in after her. Greg cradled her head in his lap, looking down at her beauty. He began to stroke her breast.

Rosa moaned and Greg took it as a signal that he could go further. He slid his hand down her body and placed his hand between her legs. He rubbed her furiously and her body strained upward to meet his hand.

Roland looked in the rear view mirror. "What the hell are you doing, Greg?"

"Just playing around."

"Knock it off. Rosa is popular with the boys, but, so far, her family's managed to keep the wolves away from her."

Greg stroked Rosa's thigh. "I'm sorry, I was out of line."

"Rosa's probably a virgin and should stay that way until she's married. Costa Ricans frown on women having sex before marriage."

"Enough, already. I get the picture."

No one spoke on the way home. Roland dropped Rosa off at her house. Greg was surprised to see it was a neat house with the grass meticulously cut and trimmed.

Seeing Greg's surprised look, Roland told him firmly, "Costa Ricans are proud, well educated people. They work hard to become successful. Rosa's father works in the coffee fields and is now a foreman and brings in a good wage. He is much respected among his people."

Greg nodded, knowing he was being chastised.

When Greg asked Rosa if he could see her again, she shook her head no. Ever since she had come home inebriated, she was only allowed to go out with her girlfriends. Greg tried to change her mind, but she held firm.

After that, Greg grew bored and called his father to ask him if he could come home. John was uncertain, but decided a month was long enough.

## Chapter 36

Katy was cleaning the house when she came across the box on the entry table. She picked it up and shook it, but nothing rattled. She saw a card affixed to the package and opened it up.

The card said "Happy birthday to a special person. Love, Patty." In a fury, Katy ripped the card into pieces and threw it in the trash.

She regarded the package as if it was a poisonous snake. She tore off the cover and stared at the heavy knit letter sweater. Katy took it out of the box and held it up. She had to admit it was large enough to accommodate Colton's broad shoulders.

She wanted to tear the sweater to bits, but a warning voice told her she'd better not. Instead, she stuffed it back into the box and crushed the lid, making sure the sweater would be wrinkled.

Katy pretended to be sick and made sure she was lying down on the sofa when Drew came home from work.

"Katy, where are you?"

"I'm in here," she said, purposely making her voice thin and wavering.

Drew rushed over to her side. "What's the matter, honey?" he asked.

Katy moaned. "I think I'm having a migraine. The pain is so bad, I'm sick to my stomach."

"I'm so sorry. I'll get you some warm milk and some Tylenol. I'll be back in a jiff."

*Yuck,* Katy thought. *I hate warm milk. Maybe I should give up my charade.*

Drew came back and placed his arm under her back, pushing her into a sitting position. He pressed the glass to her lips and made her take a drink.

Katy had all she could do not to choke, but she feigned sneezing.

Drew placed the glass on the end table. He pushed her back down on the sofa and crooned, "Rest some more. I'll be back soon to check on you." He tiptoed out of the room.

When Colton got home and found what his mother had done to his sweater. "Where is she?" he screamed. "I hate her! Dad, look what she did to my sweater!"

Drew came running and saw his son clutching the wrinkled mess of a sweater to his chest.

"This is my birthday present from Patty and she tried to ruin it!"

Drew didn't have to ask who Colton was talking about. He marched into the living room and jerked Katy off the sofa. "Get up, you phony," he hollered. "Get your jacket and get out of here! Colton and I don't want you around here!" He opened the door and shoved her out.

"Where will I go?" Katy cried.

"You can go to hell for all I care!" Drew yelled and slammed the door.

Colton felt horrible. His family was falling apart. He knew he was the cause of it. His mother smothered him and, for years, his father allowed it. *She took it too far,* Colton told himself, but it didn't stop the guilt.

## Chapter 37

A group of kids decided to have a party for the Westfield football team. Patty and Colton were invited. He wanted to wear the sweater Patty had given him, but he didn't know what to do with the wrinkled mess. He asked Patty to come over and see what she could do.

The first thing she did was place the sweater on a padded hanger. She put it on the shower rod and told Colton to leave it there while he took a shower. The steam took most of the wrinkles out, just like she thought it would.

Next, she put the garment in the dryer and set the temperature on cool for fifteen minutes. When she heard the buzzer, she shook it out and hung it outside to complete the drying.

Colton was nervous about the circumstances at home and wasn't in the mood to go to the party. He knew he had to, since he was the most popular player on the team. He fought down the urge to hurt someone. It was a cold, hard feeling that wouldn't go away.

Patty could hear the music of the party already in swing as they walked up three flights of stairs to apartment 306. When Colton opened the door, he was mobbed by teenagers. Girls hugged him and a few kissed him on the cheek.

Bruce saw Colton's sweater and bellowed. "Hey, pal, where did you get that sweater? It's awesome!"

Colton smiled at Patty, but didn't reply.

Another player asked, "What store carries those? I want one just like it!"

Colton just smiled.

"I'll bet you stole it," he said, kidding around.

Colton gave him the finger and walked over to the cooler to get Patty a beer.

After a few beers, some of the guys walked outside to smoke. They knew it was against the coach's rules, but they enjoyed one every once in a while.

Patty and Colton stood by the railing and talked to each other.

Colton felt a hard clap and a shove from behind. "What the hell?" he cried, turning around.

Greg stood there with a beer in his hand, smiling wickedly. "Hi, killer," he said.

"What did you say? You know my nickname's Cutter."

"I think killer is more appropriate myself."

Colton felt a familiar feeling wash over him. He wanted to hurt Greg badly.

Patty walked away when she saw the look on his face.

Colton put his nose in Greg's face. "Watch your filthy mouth," he growled. He picked Greg up by the collar and hoisted him over the railing.

He quickly walked over to where Patty and some other kids were singing the fight song. When the song ended, everyone dispersed, going inside to get a drink. No one noticed Greg was missing.

Much later, everyone had had too much to drink. Some guys started to leave with their best girls on their arm, while others were kissing deeply.

"How about it? Do you want to join them?" Colton asked Patty.

She reddened and punched him on the arm. "Down boy," she said laughing.

A girl screamed from downstairs and everybody ran to look. "Oh, my God!" another girl cried. "It's Greg! He must have jumped!"

"How much did he have to drink?" someone asked.

They all stared down at Greg's broken body, lying at a strange angle. His leg was under his body and blood gushed from his head.

"Call 911!" someone shouted.

Patty began to cry. "Why would he do that?" she wailed.

Colton put his arm around her waist. "Come on, honey," he said. "I'll take you home."

They were walking away from the scene when the ambulance raced by them. *I got away with another one,* Colton thought smugly.

When Patty and Colton walked into the Marlin house, her mother knew at once something was wrong. She took in Patty's swollen eyes and Colton's grave expression. "Why are you home so early?" she asked, thinking the kids had had a fight.

Patty sank into a chair. "I can't talk about it," she said flatly.

Mary looked inquiringly at Colton.

"Greg jumped off the balcony and probably killed himself," he bluntly said.

Her hands flew to her mouth. "My God! What would prompt him to do such a thing?"

Colton shrugged his shoulders and Patty broke out in more tears.

Mary lifted Patty out of the chair and cradled her in her arms. Although she could smell beer on her, she knew the gruesome scene had sobered her up. None the less, she said, "Come on, Colton. I'll fix the two of you some coffee. Maybe the warmth will make you feel better."

When the three of them were seated with their coffee, Patty's mother said, "You know the police are going to investigate Greg's attempted suicide. The chief will most likely ask everyone at the party if he was acting strange or said anything weird to anyone."

"They should," Colton said.

Patty moaned. "I don't think I can handle it."

"Sure you can. You'll do whatever you have to do," Colton told her.

## Chapter 38

The next day before game time, the players huddled together and one said, "I don't feel like playing. Greg's presence is everywhere. Even though he mostly sat on the bench, I miss him being here." They said a prayer for Greg and walked onto the field.

Even the coach's enthusiasm didn't rub off on them. The team played the game halfhearted, with the exception of Colton. He brutally tackled the opponents left and right and sacked the other teams quarterback to end the game.

The subdued cheerleaders raised their pom-poms in victory and the fans didn't rejoice as usual.

The coach called Colton aside as he walked into the locker room. "I want to talk to you," he said.

He took Colton into his office and told him to sit down. "Listen, son, I have some exciting news for you. I didn't tell you before the game because I didn't want you to get nervous like the last time. The scouts from Valparaiso were here today, scouting potential players for their team. They liked what they saw in you and I think they'll recruit you soon."

Colton's heart quickened. *Mom will be so thrilled,* he thought. Being a staunch Lutheran, she would think his success was an answer to her prayers. He forgot for a moment she wasn't living with them and wouldn't know about his good fortune.

A few days later, the coach called Colton into his office. All smiles, he handed Colton some papers.

Colton scanned them and asked, "Are these what I think they are?"

"You bet, read them over carefully."

When Colton was finished reading, he cried, "Can you believe this? My tuition will be paid for and I'll even receive money for my personal expenses!"

"Alumni are known to be generous when they want something badly enough."

Colton was overwhelmed with joy. He raised his hand and the coach gave him a high five. "Give me a pen. I want to sign it before I wake up and find out it's a dream."

Laughing, Coach Wilson handed Colton a pen.

## Chapter 39

A subdued Katy didn't fight when Drew suggested she go to a psychiatrist. Because she wanted to come back home, she acted like a docile lamb.

Drew took her to her first appointment. The receptionist greeted them and led them back to Dr. Martin's office. He introduced himself and said, "Since this is Katy's first session with me, I'd like to speak with both of you. First, tell me why you're here."

Katy began to answer, but Drew cut her off. "Let me answer your question," Drew replied. "We have a son, Colton, who is a delightful boy. Katy smothers him with affection so much that he wants to rebel. Recently, he started going out with a perfectly nice girl and Katy treated her badly. I doubt if she'll ever come back to our house again."

Katy broke in, "I didn't..." she began, but the doctor raised his hand, quieting her.

Drew began again, "Colton's girlfriend gave him a beautiful sweater for his birthday and Katy tried to ruin it. She doesn't want to share him with anyone, sometimes even me."

"What do you have to say about this, Mrs. Colby?"

"I didn't do anything except what any mother would do. He's my only child, after all."

Drew harrumphed.

"I can see why you would be protective of him, but you're obviously going too far," Dr. Martin told her.

Katy immediately struck back. "You're a stranger, what do you know?"

"This is my vocation; it's my business to find the root of your problem."

"I don't have a problem!" Katy yelled.

"See what I mean?" Drew commented.

"I don't know if I can help you if you don't cooperate. As part of your treatment, I'll have to talk to your son also."

"No!" Katy screamed.

"See how she is?" Drew asked calmly.

The doctor nodded his head yes. "I'll tell you what I think would be your best option, Mr. Colby. Take your wife home and see if she acts normal. If not, I recommend checking her into Rest Haven so she can get some help. She'll be evaluated and they'll treat her accordingly."

"I won't go!" Katy shouted.

"Yes you will, Katy," Drew said. "Either you behave or I'll have no alternative. How long will she stay there, Doctor?"

"However long it takes her to respond to the treatment. Maybe six months to a year. Some get out sooner; some cases are more difficult and require more time."

Katy wrung her hands. "You wouldn't do that to me, would you, Drew?"

"If it helps you, I will."

Katy changed her tone. "I'll try to behave, but I don't want Colton to see that hussy anymore."

"See how determined she is?" Drew asked the doctor, exasperated.

"Indeed I do." He stood up and offered Drew his hand. "It was nice meeting you. If you need me, I'm at your disposal."

Drew shook hands with the man and he and Katy left the office. She didn't utter a word all the way home.

## Chapter 40

Colton heard at football practice that Greg wasn't dead. His heart sank until a member of the team said he was in a coma and the doctors didn't know when or if he was going to wake up. When Greg hadn't responded after a week, Colton breathed a sigh of relief.

Meanwhile, John told the chief and anyone else who would listen that his son wouldn't attempt suicide. He spent every minute of every day at his bedside, willing him to regain consciousness.

The chief called everyone at the party to speak with them personally.

He talked to Patty first. She was so nervous that she began to shake when he knocked on her front door.

They sat down in the living room and the chief started questioning her. "Did you see anything out of the ordinary during the party?"

"No," Patty answered quietly. "All the kids were drinking beers and telling jokes."

"When was Greg's body discovered?"

"I don't remember exactly, but someone who left the party early found him."

The chief got up from his chair. "That's all the questions I have right now. If you think of anything else, please let me know." He looked at his list. "I'm going to see Colton Colby next."

"He was my date. I doubt if he can tell you anything more than I can."

"I see. I intend to speak with everyone who was at the party."

As soon as the chief left, Patty got on the phone and called Colton. "The chief was just here and he's on his way to see you. I thought I'd give you a heads up."

"That's okay, I've been expecting him. I'll see you later." Colton had barely hung up when the chief rang the doorbell. Colton ran to answer it because he didn't want his mother to get there first.

The chief talked to everyone at the party and all of them said the same thing. John Matthews was raising hell, contending that Greg would definitely not try to kill himself. He told the chief that an anonymous source had told him that he and Colton had an altercation at the party.

The chief talked to Colton again, trying to find out the truth.

Colton smiled. "Sure we had words. Greg was always on me about something."

"Why is that?" the chief asked.

"I think he's jealous of me. I'm a football star and he mostly sits on the bench."

The chief nodded his head, satisfied. He knew the boy would probably envy Colton's success. He decided to stop the investigation because he wasn't getting any new information.

John Matthews was the only one irate about it; everyone else was relieved the questioning was over.

## Chapter 41

Buck suddenly became aggressive. One day, he brought a dead squirrel to the doorstep. Another time, a rabbit, his jowls dripping with blood.

Katy was horrified and angrily took one of Drew's belts and whipped him with it.

When Colton heard his dog howl, he ran to see what was wrong with him. When he saw his mother with the belt in her hand, he lost control. He grabbed the belt and wiped the dog's muzzle with a wet paper towel. "Bad boy," he said when he saw the dead rabbit.

Buck looked at him as if he didn't know what he had done wrong. Colton realized that he had taught Buck to be a killer just like him. He dropped to his knees and hugged the dog. "Please try to be good," he crooned. He couldn't be sure, but he thought Buck understood him.

Colton got his leash and decided to walk him, just to see how he would react to other animals.

During the walk, Buck encountered squirrels, rabbits and chipmunks and didn't make a move toward any of them. Colton hoped the killings were over.

Colton told his father what had happened when he got home for work.

Drew stared at Buck, then at his wife. He looked her in the eye and said, "Dogs aren't human beings. I can't believe you whipped him, Katy!"

"I never want to lay eyes on that beast again!" she screamed.

After that, Colton had to be sure he fed the dog and let him out before he went to school. Katy wouldn't have anything to do with him. Drew watched her closely for other signs of mental illness.

## Chapter 42

Colton's math grade had fallen to a C and he was afraid that he would be kicked off the football team. Drew quickly hired a tutor that was recommended by the school.

The tutor was a young lady eighteen years old who had a 4.0 grade point average in her first year of college. She had straight, brown hair that fell to her shoulders and a ready smile.

The first day she came to the house, Katy opened the door and didn't want to let her in. Colton shoved his mother out of the way and led her to the den.

Katy kept interrupting, asking if he wanted a drink or some snacks. Colton looked at his mother with hatred and told her to get out and stay out. The tutor was obviously afraid of Katy and left early.

Colton stormed into the kitchen. "What is wrong with you?" he shouted. "Don't you want me to get better grades in math?"

Katy shrugged her shoulders. "I don't care if you play football anyway. It keeps you away from home too often."

"You mean away from you, don't you?" he yelled. It was all he could do to keep from backhanding his mother.

He was shaking so badly that he had to get away from her, so he called Buck and they went out to the backyard. Outside in the sunshine, he threw balls for the dog to retrieve and soon got his temper under control.

The incident was the last straw as far as Drew was concerned. He took Katy by the shoulders and shook her. "What the hell is wrong with you?" he hollered. "You don't own your son and you treat him more like a lover, for God's sake! I'll have to call the poor girl and apologize. We'll be lucky if she ever comes back here again!"

Drew went to the den and called Dr. Martin. When the doctor heard what happened, he told Drew he would call in a prescription for Katy. "See that she takes one pill every six hours. That should keep her under control. Let me know how she does."

Drew hung up the phone, hoping the medicine would do the trick.

## Chapter 43

John Matthews had just returned to Greg's room after a break in the cafeteria when he thought he saw Greg's leg move slightly. He shook his head; sure that he had imagined it. Then he saw it again.

John ran out into the hall and grabbed the first nurse he saw. "My son moved his leg!" he cried.

"Thank God," the nurse exclaimed. She told the nurse at the desk to page Dr. Ralston and then rushed into Greg's room with John to watch the motionless boy, praying for him to move again.

When the doctor arrived, he shone a light in each eye and there was a flicker of movement. Encouraged, he took a small, rubber hammer and struck Greg under the knee. There was no reaction. As he stood back and considered, Greg moaned. He ran to the boy and bent over him so he could hear him if he spoke. "Can you hear me?" he asked.

There was no answer, but the boy moved his head slightly.

The doctor was encouraged. He bent down closer. "Do you remember your fall?" he asked.

Greg nodded. "Pushed," he said softly.

"By whom?" the doctor asked.

"Cog," was the answer.

Dr. Ralston was puzzled. "Who?" he asked in a louder voice.

"Horse," Greg said plainly. His head then lolled to the side and he fell into unconsciousness.

"What did he mean by that?" the nurse asked.

"I have no idea, but we have to notify the police chief immediately. Maybe he'll have a clue as to what it means. Now, we'll let Greg rest. With any luck, this is his first step toward recovery. All we can do is wait and see."

Layton talked to Dr. Ralston in the lounge. After hearing his story, he shook his head, baffled. "Horse? As far as I know, Greg's never been around any farm animals. John detests them, so I'm sure he wouldn't allow his son near them."

"I'll call a doctor I know at the university. He specializes in this sort of thing. Maybe he can give you some insight."

"Thank you," Luke said to the doctor. "It's the only break I've had so far. I hope it helps us." He rose from his chair. "Let me know if Greg says anything else," he said, walking away.

"I will," Dr. Ralston answered.

The story of Greg's awakening made the news and when Colton heard it he broke into a cold, clammy sweat. He had to find out what Greg said. He picked up the phone and called the chief's son, Cary, who was on the football team.

Feigning joy at the good news, Colton asked him if he knew what Greg had said.

"Not really," Cary answered. "Dad's playing it close to his vest. I think I heard him say something about a horse."

"Horse?" Colton asked, pretending to be surprised. Horse sounded like he may have been trying to say Colton. "All I can say is I'm happy he's coming around. I'll see ya at practice, buddy."

Colton felt a throbbing headache coming on, so he went in the bathroom in search of an aspirin. The first thing he saw was Katy's new prescription. He noticed that she was supposed to take a pill every six hours. He wondered what would happen if she took half the bottle at one time. He smiled at the thought.

## Chapter 44

Drew arranged to have Carol, the tutor, meet his son at the school library. Colton was there with her when an announcement can over the PA system. The principal's voice said, "I regret to inform you that your classmate and friend, Gregory Matthews, passed away this morning in his sleep."

The silence was deafening.

Colton heart leapt with joy. *Saved by the bell,* he thought.

Colton brought up the subject of buying a car that night after dinner. Katy was back to cooking excellent meals and even surprising them with new recipes. Everyone was sated and Colton thought it would be a good time to broach the subject.

"Dad," he said. "I've had my driver's license for six months now, so I was wondering if you would come with me to look at cars."

Drew grinned broadly. "I've been thinking about that too, son. It's high time you have your own transportation."

"Could we go look on Saturday?" Colton asked excitedly.

"Sounds good to me."

Katy stood up abruptly from her chair. "I won't have it! My son is too young to have a car of his own!" she cried.

Colton looked at her in shock.

"Stop that, Katy!" Drew exploded. "All his friends already have one."

"He'll kill himself!" she wailed.

Buck cowered and left the room to get away from the arguing.

Drew got up and grabbed her by the shoulders. "Go upstairs and get her pills," he told Colton.

Colton obediently ran upstairs to the bathroom. On the way back down, he encountered his father hauling his screaming mother to their bedroom.

He stepped aside to let them pass and calmly walked into the kitchen. He poured a cup of coffee and then took the bottle of pills from his pocket. Colton poured half of the bottle in the cup and stirred the coffee until the pills dissolved.

He went upstairs to his parent's room and silently handed the cup to his father, who was trying to restrain Katy on the bed.

"Drink this!" Drew commanded, holding his wife's mouth open. He poured some coffee down her throat. She choked, but swallowed.

After that, she willingly drank the rest of the cup, then lay back on the pillows. "I'm so tired," she moaned. Those were the last words Katy would ever speak.

As Colton walked back to the bathroom to return the rest of the pills, he said quietly, "Sweet dreams, Mommy dearest," and calmly walked downstairs.

Colton was still sleeping the next morning when a loud siren awakened him. He ran to the window and saw an ambulance turn into his driveway. Suddenly, he remembered what he had done the night before. Acting concerned, he ran out of his room clad only in his underwear and a t-shirt. "What's happening?" he cried.

"It's your mother," Drew said. "Get out of the way. The men are bringing the stretcher up the stairs."

Colton watched as his mother was placed on the gurney and carried out the door.

Drew ran after it, shouting to Colton, "I'm riding in the ambulance. Stay home from school and I'll call you later."

He got dressed and went downstairs. He fed and watered Buck and then took him for a run.

Colton came back in and turned the television on and watched a soap opera that his mother always liked. To his credit, he felt a pang of regret.

He was reading the newspaper when the phone rang. The broken voice of his father came on the line. "The doctors pumped out your mother's stomach, but it was too late. She was pronounced dead a few minutes ago." Drew began sobbing.

"Should I come?" Colton asked.

"No, stay there. I'll want you to help me make the arrangements, I can't think clearly right now."

Colton hung up the phone, bent down and put his head between his legs. He was having trouble breathing. He hadn't thought about how his mother's death would affect his father. Colton realized he had made a mistake. Katy had been Drew's only true love and Colton had destroyed her. He hoped his father would survive the pain.

## Chapter 45

Colton missed Greg's funeral because he was helping his father make plans for his mother's service. The football team and Coach Wilson went en masse.

After it was over, they stopped at Colton's house to offer their condolences. They presented Colton and Drew with a huge peace lily. Drew was so overcome that he couldn't talk to them, but Colton put on his best act and played the grieving son.

He realized it was ironic that they had brought the one flower his mother didn't like. She always said they reminded her of funerals. Colton laughed out loud.

Drew stared at him. How could he laugh at a time like this? He decided that everyone handled grief in their own way and thought if Colton didn't laugh, he would break down and cry.

Patty and her mother brought over enough food for several days. They had meat loaf, potato salad, fried chicken, pasta salad, sliced ham, rolls and a chocolate cake.

Patty kissed Colton on the cheek and gave him a brief hug. She whispered in his ear, "I'll always be here for you. Call me when you can."

When they left, Colton thought about how sweet Patty was. She didn't deserve a monster like him.

The football season ended without Colton playing in the last two games. Everyone understood when Westfield lost.

Sympathy cards arrived at the Colby house, as many as twenty-five a day. Colton thought smugly about how much he was adored in Westfield and felt he could do no wrong.

## Chapter 46

After the funeral, Drew moped around the house. He only went to work because he needed money to exist. The mourning lasted for several months, until he came home later and later smelling of booze and perfume.

Colton was left alone and had to fend for himself. He lived on frozen dinners and delivered pizzas. Every time Colton looked in the kitchen, there was no milk or dog food for Buck. He had to beg his father for money to go to the store.

Drew grew more and more surly, missing work half of the time. In spite of himself, Colton longed for his mother's home cooked meals and even her doting ways.

One evening, Colton was making hot dogs for dinner with frozen french fries and a can of baked beans when his father walked in the door. "What are we having for dinner tonight?" he asked.

Colton looked at him with disgust. Drew hadn't eaten at home for a month. He gestured at the stove where the hot dogs were boiling and replied, 'What you see is what you get."

His father looked offended. "I don't want to eat that slop. Do you know what hot dogs are made of? Lips and snouts..."

Colton cut him off. "That's the kind of food I eat every night."

Drew's face fell, then he brightened and said jovially, "I'll tell you what, son, to make it up to you; I'll take you out to the Wagon Wheel for a huge T-bone."

Colton was going to refuse, but a solid meal sounded good. He turned off the burner and went to the closet to get his jacket. "I'm ready," he said.

In the car, Drew chattered away nonstop. Colton could care less what he was saying; he just stared out the window. He realized that they were going to opposite direction of the restaurant. "I thought we were going to the Wagon Wheel," he said.

"We are, I'm just stopping to pick someone else up on the way."

Colton's heart fell. *It was silly to think Dad wanted to spend some time with me,* he thought.

Drew drove to the poor section of town and stopped at a ramshackle house that used to be painted white, but was now a dirty gray. Its shutters were askew and the lawn looked like it hadn't been mown for a while.

Drew beeped the horn and a tall, leggy blonde Colton's age came running out of the house. She was neatly dressed in black jeans, a black and white striped t-shirt and snow white tennis shoes.

"Hi babe," Drew said as she jumped into the back seat. "You don't have to sit back there."

"It's okay, I want you and your son to sit together."

Drew pulled the car away from the curb. "Colton, this young lady is Connie," he said.

Colton looked over the seat and said, "Hi, Connie." That was all that was spoken until they pulled into the restaurant parking lot.

"I called ahead for reservations," Drew said. "It wasn't really necessary because I come here all of the time."

"Cool," Connie said. Colton now knew where his father drank.

During the meal, it was evident that Connie was invited so she could meet Colton. To Drew's dismay, he declared that he was going steady with a girl and intended to marry her one day.

Connie wasn't surprised in the least and congratulated Colton. "I have an on and off boyfriend too."

Drew didn't say anything, but he had a sour look on his face.

*Was it possible Dad didn't like Patty either?* Colton thought. He decided right then and there he had to nip his father's thoughts in the bud. The familiar warmth surged through his body and he became sexually aroused.

It wasn't long before Connie started to come on to him. She rubbed her leg against his, still carrying on a conversation without missing a beat.

Colton crossed his legs and moved over, but she didn't stop. He stood up. "I'm going to hit the john," he told his father.

When he returned, it was time to leave. The three of them got into the car and talked congenially all the way to Connie's house.

Before she got out of the car, Connie pressed a piece of paper into Colton's hand.

He thought his father didn't see it, but he was wrong. "Come sit in the front seat and let me see what that note says. I'll bet it's her phone number."

Colton crawled in the front seat and reluctantly handed the note to his father.

"Yeah, it's her number," he said laughing. "You little fox, you know how to play hard to get, don't you? That drives the girls crazy!"

"Connie's nice, but I'm not interested. Quit trying to fix me up, Dad, I've found the girl of my dreams." He didn't tell his father he had found his next victim. He knew he couldn't kill again this soon. The thought sickened him, but he knew he would have to wait a while.

## Chapter 47

The senior prom was coming up and Colton and Patty were looking forward to it. She had already picked out a formal. It was an over the shoulder style with a tight fitted bodice made of red and white dotted swiss. The skirt was full and swirled from side to side when she walked. Patty told Colton her corsage should be red roses to match her dress.

Protocol was that the senior class president and his girl lead the grand march. However, the boy had moved away suddenly and a replacement had not yet been selected.

The student body decided that they should vote on who leads the promenade. Of course, Colton was a shoe-in, beating the nearest candidate by fifty votes.

Girls flirted mercilessly with him, hoping to be his date at the prom. "I hate it when all those girls flock around you," Patty complained.

Colton kissed her on the cheek. "Honey, you know you're my one and only."

"So you say," she said doubtfully.

Colton signed his name on Patty's dance card three times to make sure he'd have her to himself at least part of the time. Other fellows quickly signed up for the rest of the dances.

Since Patty went out with Colton, she was noticed and sought after. She was gracious with all of the boys she danced with, unaware of how pretty she was. Out of the corner of her eye, she saw Colton surrounded by girls and felt a pang of jealousy.

Patty wondered how well she really knew Colton. There was something strange about him that she couldn't put her finger on. She quickly pushed the idea from her mind.

The four piece band struck up a rendition of the school's song and the cheerleaders led a cheer from the stage.

The band played Pomp and Circumstance and it was time to crown the prom king and queen. A crown was placed on Colton's head. Patty stood beside him as everyone cheered.

Some rowdy boys spiked the punch with vodka. Colton toasted everyone and Patty could tell he was getting drunk. She pulled on his arm. "Please don't drink any more, Colton," she pleaded.

He reacted angrily. "Knock it off, Patty. You're not my keeper!" he shouted.

She turned red and ran for the door. When she got outside, the wind tousled her hair, causing her updo to become unpinned. Resolutely, she took off her high heels and marched down Main Street toward home.

Behind her, she could hear a group of boys come out of the auditorium. She heard Colton's voice shouting, "Where the hell did my broad go?"

Patty walked faster, but Colton's car pulled up beside her. "Get in!" Colton demanded.

Patty ignored him and kept walking. Colton screeched to a halt and jumped out of the car. He roughly grabbed her arm and shoved her into the front seat.

Patty was openly crying and she pressed herself against the passenger door to get as far away from him as possible.

Colton's mouth was set in anger and he pressed down on the accelerator. The needle on the speedometer rose to seventy-five miles an hour. The old car shuddered and shook, unable to handle that much speed.

A tire blew out and Patty screamed. The car slid sideways and hit a tree. There was a screech of metal and then all was silent.

A squad car saw the wreckage and came to an abrupt halt. He managed to open Colton's door and pull the shaken boy out of it. Seeing it was Colton Colby, the football star, he became alarmed.

He gently placed him in the tall grass and ran back to the car. He tried to open the passenger door, but it was too damaged.

A car braked and the driver ran over. "Can I help you, officer?" He saw what the policeman was trying to do and ran back to his car to get a crowbar. They inserted it between the door and the frame and the door screeched open.

The girl inside was unconscious and had an open gash on her forehead. Her arm was twisted at an unusual angle and she looked in serious condition. Knowing he shouldn't move her, the officer ran to his car and called for an ambulance.

The other man was pacing outside the wreckage. "I checked for a pulse!" he cried. "I couldn't find one!"

The ambulance arrived and the attendant gently lifted Patty onto a stretcher. Minutes later, the ambulance took off with sirens wailing.

The two men rushed to the other side of the wrecked car. Colton was sitting up, dazed. "What happened?" he asked.

"You've had a bad accident. How do you feel?"

"Sore all over. I must have hit the steering wheel; my chest feels like a sledge hammer hit it."

"Do you think you can walk?"

"Yeah, I think so."

"Okay," the officer said and helped him to his feet.

Colton stood unsteadily. "Where's Patty?" he asked, looking around.

"The ambulance took her to the hospital."

"I want to see her!" Colton cried.

"All in good time," the officer said, placing his hand on Colton's shoulder. When he did, he could smell alcohol on Colton's breath. *Good Lord,* he thought. *The kid's been drinking!* Then he remembered it was prom night and he decided not to give him a breathalyzer. He would take him home and let his father put him to bed.

The officer turned to the other man. "Thanks for your help. Write down your name and address in case I have to get in touch with you."

"I'm glad I was driving by. I hope the poor girl is alright."

Colton gave the man a sharp look, but didn't say anything.

"Come on, son. I'll help you to the squad car. I'll take you home. If you start feeling bad, go directly to the hospital."

"I will, sir, thank you," Colton said as he hobbled to the car with the officer's help.

## Chapter 48

The front door to Colton's house was unlocked when the officer tried it, so he helped Colton into the living room. He was appalled at what he saw. Newspapers were strewn on the floor and beer cans were tossed at random around the room.

The officer could see in the kitchen where the mess was even worse. Soiled dishes were piled on the counter and catsup stains dripped down the cupboards. "Where's your father?" he asked quietly.

Colton hung his head. "I don't know. He isn't home much lately."

The officer thought fast. He was seeing a retired nurse who took care of sick people in their homes as a way of making extra money. "Where's the phone?" he asked Colton.

He pointed to the one on the wall in the kitchen.

The officer dialed a number. "Hi Gwen, I've got a situation here I think you can help with." He went on to explain the circumstances of Colton's injuries and the sad condition of the Colby home.

"I'll be right there," she stated.

The officer started to rattle off the address, but Gwen cut him off and said, "I know where it is, I'm on my way."

A half hour later he heard a car door slam.

Gwen went directly to Colton who was sitting on the couch, staring off into space. She took off his shirt and saw his chest was black and blue. She felt his rib cage and said, "He should have an x-ray tomorrow. He undoubtedly has some cracked or broken ribs."

She reached into her bag and took out a stethoscope and listened intently. She nodded, satisfied. "Except for his racing heart, his vitals are fine. However, he'll be hurting tomorrow. Where are your night clothes, son?"

"In my bedroom," Colton replied in a voice close to a whisper.

"Go to his room, Max, and find something for him to wear. Then take him up there and help him get dressed. Call me when you're finished and I'll sedate him."

After a while, Gwen came back into the living room. "He's finally asleep, but the pain will wake him in a few hours. Where is his father anyway?"

Max shrugged. "Colton doesn't know. The man's gone off the deep end since his wife died. He's barely hanging onto his job and look at the sordid conditions he and Colton are living in."

Gwen looked around and shook her head. "I know what I'll be doing for the rest of the night."

Max walked over to her and took her in his arms. "You're the best, honey," he said.

Gwen gave him a quirky smile. "I know," she agreed.

Colton had horrible dreams all night. He tossed and turned, causing a wrenching pain. The faces of the girls he murdered floated in front of his eyes, including an extra one. Looking closer, he recognized it as Patty. A scream tore out of his throat and he sat up in bed.

Gwen came running when she heard his outcry. "What's wrong?" she asked.

Huge tears were running down Colton's face and he was sobbing uncontrollably.

"Now, now, it's alright," Gwen said soothingly.

"No it's not!" Colton hollered. "I want to call the hospital and check on Patty!"

"They won't give you any information. You're not a relative."

"That's bullshit! Take me over there!"

"Calm down, I'll make the call for you after I bring you some hot cocoa to warm you up. Later, when you get your x-rays, you can see her for yourself."

Colton was pacified for the moment, so Gwen left the room to get the cocoa. When she returned, Colton was out of bed trying to put on his jeans. He had one pant leg half way up and was struggling to stay upright.

Gwen put the cup down and gently pushed Colton on the bed. He winced with pain. "Here, let me help you," she said, pulling the jean legs up to his knees. "You can manage from there. Before you put a clean t-shirt on, go into the bathroom and wash up. That will have to do until later when I help you take a shower."

Gwen left the room to call the hospital. She didn't think she'd like the report she would get.

"Fifth floor nurses' station," a woman answered.

"This is Gwen Radar, I worked there as a nurse for many years."

"Oh, yes, Gwen, I remember you. What can I do for you?"

"I'm checking on the status of Patty Marlin, who was brought in last night. She was in a serious car accident."

There was a long pause. "I'm sorry, Gwen, Patty Marlin was brought in DOA."

Gwen's heart sank. How on earth was she going to tell Colton? Shaken, she replied, "Thank you. Do her parents know?"

"Yes, they've been here. They insisted on seeing the body. Mrs. Marlin had to be sedated before we let her go home. She went into shock."

Gwen was heartbroken because she was afraid of what Colton would do when he heard the news.

Just then, Colton hobbled into the room. He didn't notice the spotless kitchen, he was too agitated. "How's Patty?" he asked anxiously.

"Well..." Gwen began.

Colton broke in. "I can tell by your expression that something's wrong."

Gwen went over and gave him a hug. "I'm so sorry, Colton. She didn't make it."

"No!" Colton screamed. He dropped his head in agony. "It's all my fault," he lamented. "I was driving, for God's sake!"

"The car had a blown tire, that's what caused the wreck."

Colton dropped to his knees and hugged Buck fiercely. "I've lost my Patty," he moaned, dropping his head onto the dog's soft fur.

The door banged open and a disheveled Drew walked into the room. He took in the scene and asked, "What's all the hullabaloo about?"

Gwen gave him a dirty look. "If you had been here last night to console your son, you wouldn't have to ask."

"Nothing can be that bad."

"Oh yes it can, you of all people should know that. You've been acting like a jerk ever since your wife died."

"Who the hell are you? That's none of your business!"

"I'm Gwen Radar and I've been here all night cleaning up your filthy house. Come into the living room and I'll tell you the whole sordid story."

She pulled him forcefully into the other room. "Sit down and be quiet." she ordered. "When I'm finished, I'm sure you'll have something profound to say."

Drew kept his mouth shut and didn't interrupt Gwen's horrible story. When she was finished, he got up abruptly from his chair and ran to Colton. "Are you hurt, son?" he cried.

"Nothing that won't heal," Colton replied. "But Patty wasn't so lucky," he added bitterly.

Drew knelt in front of him. "Please forgive me, Cutter. I know I haven't taken your mother's death well. I'm terribly sorry and I'll make it up to you, I promise. I know you won't believe me, but the shock will fade in time. The important thing is to get on with your life. After all, you're still living."

Gwen, listening to the conversation from the living room, decided it was time to leave. It sounded like things would finally go well at the Colby house. Little did she know that Colton's agony was just beginning.

# Chapter 49

While Colton lay around the house recovering from his injuries, the Marlins were arranging Patty's funeral. Colton had sent them a sympathy card, but didn't have the guts to go see them. He had written "I'm so sorry. I'll miss her" on the card and ended it with "I'll see you soon" but Colton hadn't gotten up the courage to face them.

To make things worse, the Westfield Gazette ran the story of the accident on the front page, including a picture of Patty. The TV station reported the story too, so Colton couldn't spend his endless hours at home watching the tube.

Sympathy cards by the dozen came to the Colby house too, but Colton threw them on the table without opening them. The dream he had after the accident lingered. Was God trying to punish him by adding Patty's face to the others? Colton hung his head in shame. "I killed her too, but in a different way," he cried to himself. He raised his face and prayed for forgiveness, even though he had never prayed in his life.

The days passed and Colton's black and blue chest finally returned back to normal. The days stretched before him and he was bored to death. If it hadn't have been for the long, solitary walks with Buck, he would have gone crazy.

Drew tried to think of something to do to bond with him. He didn't like tennis and he barely tolerated golf. Football was his game, but he didn't play anymore. He knew if he tried to play with Colton, he'd be laid flat in no time.

He thought about his friends that were buying guns for protection. Even though Buck was a great watch dog, Drew decided to purchase a gun for himself. He decided to buy Colton a pistol too. That way, they could go to the shooting range together.

At first, Colton balked at the idea, but when Drew came home with two pistols and handed one to him, he changed his mind. He took the small, silver weapon in his hand and looked it over. "This gun isn't very big, is it?" he asked his father.

"No, but it will do the trick if the target is thirty yards or less away."

"When are we going to the range? I want to learn how to shoot it."

"Soon, first I'll show you how to load it and clean it. A friend showed me how to do it."

Colton's first time at the range was a disaster. He learned the proper way to stand. A large cardboard target in the shape of a man was hung from the ceiling for him to shoot at.

He stood as he was told and fired at the target. The loud report made him jump and he missed the target altogether.

His father bent over in a fit of laughter. "They should have made the target six feet eight and two hundred and fifty pounds. Try again."

Colton was embarrassed, but he got into position and tried again. He'd be damned if he wouldn't show his father he could do it. Colton fired and this time he held the gun steady. The bullet hit the target in the leg.

"That's better," the instructor said. "That shot would certainly disable an intruder, but next time aim higher." He looked at Drew. "It's your turn now."

He stepped up to the shooting line oozing confidence and fired a series of shots. All but one hit the area around the target's heart.

"I see you've used a gun before," the instructor said.

"Not for many years and not with a pistol. My father took me squirrel hunting when I was a kid. The rifle I held was almost bigger than I was."

"Okay, Colton, try one more shot and we'll call it a night. I don't want you to learn anything but the basics the first night."

Drew winced when he had to pay fifty dollars for the lesson. When they got in the car, Drew said quietly to Colton, "I flat out can't afford fifty dollars a lesson. I'll tell you what; we'll put a row of tin cans on the fence in the backyard and we can practice there. That way, it won't cost us a dime."

"You know, Dad, I've been thinking about getting a summer job. You could use the money for household expenses and I'd like to replace my old car. I'll need a car at college. I can't walk everywhere. Besides, it's an expensive school and I'm sure everyone has a car. Thank God I have a full scholarship or I couldn't put my foot in one of the dorms."

Drew laughed and said, "Don't worry, son. You'll make a name for yourself on the football field and the alumni will fall all over you."

"I hope so," Colton said, suddenly unsure of himself. "Maybe I'd be better off going to a small school where I could be a big fish in a small pond. I'm afraid I'll get lost in a big school."

Drew patted Colton's thigh. "Don't worry, Cutter, you'll do just fine."

## Chapter 50

The next week, Colton saw a help wanted sign at Sanderson's Wrecking Yard. The job sounded good to Colton. He could wear his jeans and get some exercise too. He had to keep himself in shape for the next football season.

When Colton went in to fill out the application, it asked what kind of experience he had. He thought, then wrote "No experience, but willing to learn. I need a summer job to buy a car." When he finished the application, he handed it to the large, burly man sitting at the desk.

"Sit down," the man growled. The manager glanced at the application and frowned. "No experience, huh?"

"No sir."

He scanned the paper again and smiled. "I know who you are now. I go to all of Westfield's football games. You're the best. I hear you're going to tear down the goalposts at Valparaiso." He stood up and extended his hand. "Welcome aboard, son," he said.

Colton was given the cushy job of cleaning out the interiors of the wrecked cars that could be fixed. His face got white and he ran to the restroom to throw up when he saw his old car, but the feeling passed when they moved it to the pit to be crushed. He couldn't look at the car where Patty died, so he stayed away from that end of the lot.

Colton worked on a 2006 car that had a smashed in front end. The rest of the car was in good condition. He immediately fell in love with it. The odometer read 30,000 miles and he liked the red paint job.

After the body shop worked on it, the manager came out to see the results. "She's a beauty!" he exclaimed. "The car should bring in a dandy price."

Colton looked desolate. He really wanted that car.

Seeing the expression on the boy's face, the manager laughed. "You'd like to own this one, wouldn't you, son?"

Colton's face flushed, but he replied honestly, "I know I can't afford it, but that doesn't stop me from wanting it. I have an insurance check for eight hundred dollars and if you keep half of my wages, I can pay off a chunk of it before I leave."

The manager looked at Colton seriously. "I'll see what I can do," he said and walked away.

Unknown to Colton, Mr. Sanderson told the story to the Chamber of Commerce and checks came rolling in from businesses in Westfield. Most of the town wanted to help their football hero.

In all, Mr. Sanderson raised five thousand dollars. With the insurance check, the wreckage yard would take in fifty eight hundred dollars without dipping into Colton's wages. He was very proud of himself when he asked Colton to sign the title. He saw the tears in the boy's eyes and patted him on the shoulder. "Take your time insuring it," he said. "The temporary tag is ours and our insurance will cover it. Don't mail in the title until you're ready."

"I don't know how to thank you," Colton said.

"The people of this town want to thank you for putting our little village on the map."

Colton wanted to hug him, but instead he said, "I'll work my butt off for you, weekends included."

Mr. Sanderson nodded and Colton kept his promise, working weekends all summer.

## Chapter 51

Near the end of one day, Connie sashayed over to Colton. "I heard you were working here," she said seductively.

"Well, hello," Colton replied. He looked at her generous breasts and tight behind and that old familiar feeling raced from his thighs to his groin. *What a pleasure it would be to do her,* he thought. He tried with all his might to push the idea away, but the feeling was too strong and he succumbed to it. "What are you doing tonight?" he asked. "I bought a new car and I want to take it for a ride."

"I'd love that," she crooned.

"It's a deal. I'll meet you here at eight."

"Why here?"

"I have some paperwork to do in the office and I should be done around that time."

Connie shrugged. "Okay, baby, if you say so. I'm feeling hot already!" She winked at Colton and said, "See ya."

Colton went home to have dinner with his father. On the way, he stopped and got some beef chow mein.

Drew's eyes lit up when he saw it. "I've had a craving for Chinese, how did you know?"

"A little birdie told me," Colton replied.

The two of them ate until the whole carton was empty. "Bless you, son, that was a terrific meal," Drew said.

Colton stood up from the table. "I'm going to take Buck for a short walk. After that, I have to go back to Sanderson's to finish something up. I should be home by ten at the latest."

"That's fine with me," Drew said. "I have a hot date."

*Here we go again,* Colton thought, but what the hell? He'd be going to college soon.

He ran to his room and retrieved his gun, making sure it was loaded. He placed it in the glove compartment and drove to Sanderson's to meet Connie.

She stood outside the locked fence, looking like a whore in short shorts and a low cut shirt.

Colton pulled up and rolled down his window. "Get in!" he hollered.

Connie teetered over in her spike heels and jumped in the car. "This car is awesome!" she exclaimed, cracking her gum loudly.

"Get rid of the gum, baby. We're going to have a drink and then we're going to lover's lane to make out."

Connie was so stupid, she laughed at him. "'Lover's lane'? That sounds like something from the sixties."

"Just kidding, I meant the place where all the kids go to make out." He reached in the backseat and came up with a cheap bottle of vodka. He unscrewed the cap and lifted it to his lips, pretending to take a drink.

He handed it to Connie and she took a huge gulp before she handed it back. "Isn't this fun?" she trilled. She reached in her tiny shoulder bag for a cigarette.

Colton placed his hand over hers. "No you don't, not in my new car. Let's get out so you can smoke."

"It's chilly out there."

*Then you should have worn something warmer,* he thought, but he took off his sweater and said, "Here you go."

"My hero!" she exclaimed.

Colton wanted to backhand her, but he handed her the vodka bottle and said, "Drink up; the booze will warm you up."

She took two large drinks and handed the bottle back.

"Get out of the car, honey," he urged.

Connie struggled a bit getting out, but finally made it.

Colton walked over to her and pulled her body to his. Her full breasts pressed against his chest and he rubbed his finger up and down her cleavage.

"Oh," Connie said. "Don't stop."

Instead, Colton backed away and handed her the vodka bottle. As she brought the bottle to her lips, he extracted a key from his pocket and unlocked the padlock holding the heavy chain together. It fell to the ground with a clank and the metal gates parted.

"What are you doing?" Connie asked, already slurring her words.

"I'm going to take you into the office where there's a nice, soft couch to lie on."

She giggled. "I can't wait." Connie staggered through the fence and Colton ran back to the car. "Where are you going? Don't leave me with all these old wrecks, they're creepy!"

"I'll be right back, I forgot my jacket." Colton opened the glove compartment and stuffed the gun in the waistband of his jeans. He pulled his jacket on and hurried back to Connie, who was shifting nervously from one foot to another.

"Let's get out of here!" she wailed. "I don't like it!"

Colton took her by the arm and led her in the direction of the office. "See? There's a nightlight where we're headed."

Connie relaxed and let her body slump against his.

*Shit,* Colton thought. *I don't want her to be too drunk. I want to see the terror in her eyes.* He pretended to get keys from his pocket, but pulled out the gun instead.

"What's that?" Connie cried, cowering against the wall.

"Relax," he said sharply. "I want to make sure there are no intruders around."

Her lips made a perfect 'o', but she didn't reply.

Colton roughly pushed her into the light coming from the window.  He pulled her to him and kissed her deeply.

"Do me," she muttered.

He raised the pistol and shot her in the leg.

Connie screamed in terror and clutched the gaping hole the bullet had made.

Colton fired again and this time the bullet hit her upper arm.

The girl was wailing now, her hands trying to cover both wounds at once.

Colton laughed.  "Don't you like me now, honey?"

She dropped her hands and backed away from him.  "You're a monster!" she screamed.

Colton laughed again.

"I'll do anything you want me to," she begged.  "Please don't shoot me anymore, I can't stand the pain!"

Colton was enjoying himself.  He shot her one more time in the stomach and coldly watched as she fell to the ground.  As he looked at her face, her eyes opened wide in horror, then with a small puff of breath, the life went out of her.

Colton felt the usual rush and he climaxed in his jeans.  He grabbed Connie by the arms and dragged her across the parking lot to a pile of cars that were going to be crushed.

One of the cars had a bashed in trunk, but Colton was able to open it about a foot, just enough to push Connie's body inside.  He had to shove several times because one of her arms refused to go in.  Without giving it a thought, he broke the arm by slamming it on the bumper.  He closed the trunk with a screech of metal.

Colton raced to the gate, knowing he had spent too much time there.  The police patrolled the yard regularly.  He was almost to the gate when he saw a pair of headlights coming around the corner, approaching at a high speed. He ducked back into the yard and hid behind a large tree.

After the car passed, Colton jumped into action. Leaving the gate unlocked, he ran to his car and started the engine. He quickly drove away without turning on the lights.

He saw headlights in the rear view mirror and knew this time it was the police. Luckily, there was a warehouse ahead with a road leading to it. Colton pulled into it and killed the engine. He sat there breathing heavily as the squad car paused in front of the yard and shined the spotlight around the perimeter. The car made a u-turn and drove away.

Scared by the close call, Colton took the back roads all the way home. *Was it really worth it?* he asked himself. He then remembered the feeling of ecstasy and decided it was.

The next day when Colton came to work, the other men were standing in a group in front of the office. Colton parked his car and jogged over to them. "What's up?" he asked.

"Some vagrant broke into the gate last night. He must have needed a place to sleep," the manager said angrily. He held up a partial bottle of vodka. "He even left his booze behind. If there wasn't so much sand in the bottle, I'd be tempted to take a swig right now."

Everyone laughed.

"Well, let's get to work, you guys. I'm not going to bother reporting this to the police. After all, nothing was taken."

## Chapter 52

On his last day of work, the other workers threw Colton a small party. Mr. Sanderson praised Colton on a job well done and presented him with a check which included a generous bonus. He looked at the amount with surprise. "Thank you, sir," he said politely.

"Good luck on the football field at Valpo!" the manager said.

A keg of beer was set up and everyone helped themselves to a glass. Colton drank two beers, then left the group. All of them were enjoying the party, forgetting why they had it in the first place.

Mr. Sanderson left his men and patted Colton on the back. "I hope you come back to work for me next summer," he said.

"I'll call you as soon as I get back to town. Have a good one, Mr. Sanderson," he said and walked to his car.

He drove directly home and packed his suitcase. Buck followed him, seeming to sense he was leaving. Before Colton left, he knelt down and hugged his dog. He ran his fingers though his hair. "I'll miss you, boy, but there's no way you can come along."

Colton got in the car and drove out of Westfield. He had money in his pocket and would take his time driving to Indiana. He planned on taking a full week to get there. He thought briefly of his father, but the note he left should be sufficient. He still didn't feel close to him, but as a good son, he would keep in touch.

## Chapter 53

The grounds of Valparaiso were amazing. There was green grass, fall flowers and large brick buildings everywhere Colton looked. He parked his car in front of his dorm, where he saw other guys unloading their gear.

Colton entered the building and walked up to the front desk to check in. The woman welcomed him warmly. "Mr. Colby, you'll be bunking with Jeff Becker in room 103. Here's a map showing the layout of the campus. Welcome to Valpo."

Colton was handed a brochure listing the time of services at the chapel. He noted there was an eight o'clock service every morning.

He had never had a close male friend except for Alvin, so he was nervous about meeting Jeff Becker.

When he entered the small living area, an inner door opened and a slim, blonde guy about nineteen years old grinned at Colton. "So you're the famous Colton Colby!" he welcomed him. "I'm honored to share these humble quarters with you."

Colton liked him already. "Nice to meet you," he said.

"Let me help you with your stuff," Jeff said. "We can put it in your bedroom."

Colton looked at him quizzically.

"We have separate bedrooms. Don't worry, I like my privacy too."

Colton's room had a double bed, an easy chair and a desk. Blinds covered the one window. "You can hang your clothes in the closet," Jeff said, pointing at a door in the corner of the room.

Colton flopped on the bed. "It feels great! Almost like my bed at home."

Jeff laughed. "Come on, I'll show you the rest of the abode," he said. Colton followed him back out to the living room.

"This is our only communication with the world," he said, indicating a fifteen inch TV that had seen better days.

Adjoining the living room was a small cupboard, a sink and a small counter with a microwave on it. "The mini fridge is under the counter. It only holds a six pack of beer, milk and butter. I exist on frozen dinners, fast food and pizza delivery. There's a cafeteria on campus, but the food sucks."

Jeff opened the refrigerator and took out two beers. He handed one to Colton. "Let's sit down and shoot the breeze. We should get to know each other."

Jeff sat down on the sofa and angled himself with one leg underneath him.

Colton pushed a bed pillow with a wrinkled cover aside and sat down.

"I come out here and watch TV when I can't sleep," Jeff explained. "I keep the volume low, so it shouldn't wake you up. Oh, I forgot to tell you, there's a coin laundry down the hall."

"Where's the john?"

"That's the problem; the shower and the crapper are just down the hall. We have to share it with six other guys."

Colton frowned.

"I know," Jeff said. "It takes a while to get used to. On the bright side, you can shower in the locker room after football practice or games. Any questions?"

"Yeah, where's the phone?"

"Down the hall too. What else?"

Colton handed him the schedule of church services and raised his eyebrows.

"You're at a Lutheran school, remember? We're all required to attend church each morning before class."

Colton moaned. "My mother was churchy, but Dad wasn't, so I very rarely attended church."

"Me too, but I'm learning," Jeff said affably. "Listen, I'm going to jump in the shower now while no one's around. I do it late in the day instead of the morning because if you're not one of the first ones, all the hot water's gone."

"Okay," Colton said. "Can I come with you?"

"Sure, there's two shower stalls."

After Colton had showered and put on clean clothes, he felt refreshed. "What are you going to do for dinner?" he asked Jeff.

"Heck, why don't we jump in my car and run down to Mac's Diner? They offer about anything you'd want."

Jeff's car was a brand new, red Porsche. Colton was taken by surprise when he saw it. "Man, where did you get such a hot car?" he asked.

Jeff shrugged. "I got it from my parents for high school graduation."

"Oh," was all Colton could say.

"Almost all the kids here are rich," Jeff said. "My father's a doctor and my mother's a stockbroker. They didn't have much time for me. We live in a huge house in Waukegan, Illinois, not far from Chicago."

"I'm just a country boy," Colton said. "I live in a small ranch house in Westfield, Georgia. My dad works at a paper mill and my mom's dead."

"I'm sorry, buddy," Jeff said.

During dinner, Colton told him the only way he could afford to go to Valpo was that he had a full football scholarship. "They even gave me some spending money," Colton said proudly.

"You'd better watch your Ps and Qs. The alumni will expect you to perform after they've spent all that money on you."

"I'll give them want they want," Colton said confidently. "When I played football at home, they called me a 'big, bad, killing machine'."

Jeff laughed. "We're an odd couple, but I think we'll do great together. After all, opposites attract, don't they?"

## Chapter 54

The next morning, they went to church service together. Colton almost went to sleep during the service because his mind was on other things. When the pastor started preaching about sin and corruption, Colton felt he was talking directly to him. He felt a pang of regret, but quickly pushed his gruesome memories from his mind. He was relieved when the pastor gave the benediction and the service was over.

From church, they walked to the gym where orientation was held. There were about fifty students attending, a mixture of girls and boys. Jeff waved at some of them and introduced Colton to a few others.

Everyone seemed to have heard of him and he felt the elation he had felt in Westfield. After the meeting was over, the students lined up at a table to receive the time and locations of their classes.

On the way back to the dorm, Jeff asked Colton what he was majoring in.

He shrugged his shoulders and said, "English, I guess. I have to maintain a B average if I want to play football."

"I'll help you all I can," Jeff said.

"Thanks, but I'm taking English Lit, a speech class and Contemporary Writing. I think I can scrape by in those."

"Good luck, the scholastic program isn't easy here."

"All I care about is getting back on the football field."

"The football coach is no pushover either," Jeff warned.

"I guess I'll find out tomorrow," Colton said, not a confident as he sounded.

## Chapter 55

Colton reported to football practice at four o'clock the next day. He immediately noticed a difference from his high school practices. For one thing, all of the players were huge, most of them about two hundred fifty pounds. Colton, at two hundred, was the smallest one of the lot. He told himself since he weighed less, he would be faster than the other players.

During scrimmage, Colton got knocked around and finally Coach Paul Hogan ordered him to sit on the bench. "Son, I know you came here with good recommendations, but the truth of the matter is, you've gotten out of shape during the summer. Starting tomorrow, hit the exercise room. Lift weights, do whatever you have to do to develop your muscles."

"Okay, I'll start tonight."

"Work out for a week and then report back to practice. I'll reevaluate you then. We have our first game coming up soon and it's going to be tough. We can't have any weak links on the squad."

Colton was dismayed. He was used to being a big cheese with all the adoration that went with it. "Yes, sir," he said, even though he was seething with anger. He was suddenly lonesome for Westfield and decided he would call home after he ate a quick sandwich.

Drew answered on the first ring.

"Hi, Dad, it's Colton. How's everything at home?"

"Good to hear from you, son. How are you doing at school? Have you gotten out on the football field yet?"

"Yeah, I'm doing great," Colton lied.

"That's my boy."

"Dad, I miss Buck. How is he?"

There was a long silence on the line. "I'm sorry, Cutter, he ran away last week."

"What?" Colton shouted. "How could that happen?"

"Well, I let him out one morning and forgot to let him back in. When I got home that night, he was gone."

"God damn it, how could you do such a thing? Put an ad in the paper, offer a reward, do what you have to do to get him back!"

"Okay, I'll do what I can. Call me back in a few days and I'll let you know what happened."

"You do that!" Colton shouted and hung up the phone. He wanted to go home, but he knew if he did, he'd mess everything up. He went to the gym and worked off his anger.

When he got back to the dorm, he snapped at Jeff and went into his bedroom, slamming the door behind him.

He tossed and turned all night and missed his first two classes in the morning. With an effort, he got dressed and attended his speech class, where he didn't pay any attention to what the professor was saying.

## Chapter 56

In Westfield, Buck was lonely and confused. He missed Colton and couldn't understand why he wasn't around anymore. The dog went out in the woods and scratched around a pile of leaves to make himself a bed. He went back to the house every day, but there was never any food or water for him. His bowls were empty.

He went back to the house one more time, but nothing had changed. Forlornly, he trotted away.

Colton anxiously called his father two days later. "Is Buck back yet?" he asked.

"No, I haven't seen him."

"Did you put an ad in the paper like I told you to?"

"No, I didn't want to spend the money on a useless dog. He was just another mouth to feed."

"I hate you for this and will never forgive you. I'll be home in a few days and I'll find him myself!"

Colton told Jeff there was a death in the family and he had to go back home for the funeral. He also notified all his professors and Coach Hogan. The coach wasn't happy and told Colton he would miss some valuable time and he would have to bench him when he got back. He didn't want to give up his chance for making the team, but Colton knew what he had to do.

He hastily threw some clothes in his duffle bag and started the long journey home.

Meanwhile, Buck was scrounging up food wherever he could find it. Sometimes, people would leave their pet's dish outside and one time he went on a man's property and killed a chicken. The man saw him and fired his shotgun. Buck ran and luckily the shot missed him.

Later that day, a man spotted him sitting on the edge of his property. He could see the dog was starving, his ribs were showing, but he could see that he was a thoroughbred. He assumed it was someone's pet that had run away. "Come here, boy," he called.

At first Buck hesitated, then he walked slowly to him. The man put out his hand and pet the dog. "I wonder what your name is," he said. "How about if I call you Loner? Come on, I have a steak bone and some leftover cat food in the house. First, I'll get you some water."

Buck watched the man go into the house and sat down on his haunches to wait for his return.

The man brought out an aluminum cake pan filled with water. Buck looked at it with interest, but didn't move.

"Come on, boy, I know you're thirsty."

The man's voice was pleasant, so Buck walked over to the pan and drank greedily.

The man brought out a bowl of cat food, which Buck ate quickly. He threw a bone at the dog and went in to read the paper. He looked at the lost animal column, but there was no mention of a Shepard. "What am I going to do with you?" he asked.

Buck perked up his ears and stared at him.

The man thought for a minute and picked up his cell phone. "Barb," he said. "You need a watch dog. I have just the one for you. I'll put him in the truck and bring him over."

Colton was on the outskirts of Westfield. He stopped at the house, but didn't see any sign of Buck. He drove block after block, searching for him.

On the edge of town, he happened to glance at a small bungalow. In the backyard, Buck was playing with a boy and girl about seven years old. He stopped the car and started to get out. The dog perked up his ears and stared at the car. Colton wanted to get out and claim him, but he didn't know what he would do with him. He couldn't take him to school and his father clearly wouldn't take care of him. Colton drove away slowly. "Buck found himself a good home," he told himself, eyes misting. He stepped on the accelerator and started the long drive back to school.

## Chapter 57

On the way back, the feeling of need came over him. He hadn't felt it for a long time, but it was persistent. He squelched it with an effort. He was sure something would present itself soon.

When he got back to campus, he parked the car and ran up to his room. He walked in on Jeff and a pretty, petite girl necking on the couch. They jumped apart when he entered the room. "I'm sorry," he said and backed out the door.

"Come back here," Jeff called. "I want to introduce you to my girlfriend. Polly, this is Cutter, my roommate."

"Hi there," Colton said, noting her curly blonde hair and big blue eyes.

"Jeff's told me so much about you," she said smiling.

Colton plopped down on the easy chair. "What's for dinner?" he asked.

"See?" Jeff said, poking Polly in the ribs. "I told you he was a bottomless pit."

They agreed to cheeseburgers and french fries, so Jeff and Polly left to pick up the order.

While they were gone, Colton took a shower and put on clean clothes. He felt like a new man.

Colton flirted outrageously with Polly and she flirted back with a twinkle in her eyes. He realized she'd make a great victim. He would enjoy watching her squirm. He chastised himself. He didn't want to hurt Jeff, so he put the idea out of his mind.

When Jeff returned from taking Polly home, he was angry. "What the hell did you think you were doing, flirting with my girlfriend?"

"Simmer down, Jeff, I was just playing around."

"Don't do it again or you'll regret it," he threatened.

"Never fear, I'm not really interested in girls."

"You aren't gay, are you?"

"Of course not, you lame brain. I just haven't found the right girl yet."

Satisfied, Jeff said, "Okay, I'm sorry. Let's call a truce and we'll never mention it again, okay?"

Colton nodded. "Agreed," he said and gave Jeff a high five.

## Chapter 58

The team welcomed Colton back warmly. "Okay, let's go!" the coach shouted.

The players lined up and the scrimmage began. Colton seemed to be everywhere on the field. He tackled one player after the other without tiring.

Because it was an unusually warm day, Coach Hogan stopped the practice early. "Nice going, fellows," he told the team. "If the weather's cooler tomorrow, we'll be out here longer."

Just as Colton was leaving the locker room, the coach stopped him. "I looked at your records and see that you're an English major. I'm in charge of the school newspaper. Why don't you join us?"

Colton hesitated. "It sounds like fun, but I don't think I have the time."

"The paper only comes out once a month and the alumni would be delighted. It never hurts to keep them happy," he said, winking at Colton.

"When you put it that way, how can I refuse?"

The coach took him to the press room where several students were working on the paper. "Guys, this is Colton Colby. He's going to join our staff."

"Oh, great," one boy mumbled under his breath.

A girl smiled at him. "I'm Jackie," she said. "The sour puss over there is Ted, but he's a hell of a writer."

Colton gave Ted a big smile. He was determined to kill him with kindness.

"Colton is tuckered out from practice right now, but he'll join you in a couple of days."

"See you later, tiger," Jackie said, batting her eyes.

Colton grinned and said, "See ya." She wasn't Colton's type, but was a good candidate for the little caper he was planning.

That evening, the opportunity presented itself. He told Jeff he was going for a run. He was running in the woods that circled the campus when he rounded a corner and ran into Jackie. She was walking a tan dog. He stopped when he approached her. "Hi, Jackie. Are you out walking your dog?"

"Yeah, I rescued him from the pound yesterday."

"He's a big brute, isn't he?"

"Yeah, his name is Tiger. I think he's a pit mix."

"I had a Shepard once, but I had to give him up when I came here."

"I'm sorry, that must have been hard."

"It was. You don't stay on campus, do you? You can't have a dog in the dorms."

"I live in the Haywood subdivision with my parents."

Colton watched as the dog lunged on his leash, acting nervous and agitated. He walked over to the dog and Colton began to shake its head from side to side. The dog growled and snapped at him viciously.

"Don't do that!" Jackie screamed. "You're making him crazy!"

"I used to do that with my Shepard all the time. We're just playing," he said, knowing better.

After Colton had the dog worked up, he stood and pretended to trip. He banged into Jackie, causing her to fall.

"Help me up!" she squealed.

Colton stared at her as he pushed her to her backward and straddled her. Jackie was turned on, thinking he was going to kiss her. Instead, he started pummeling her.

"Stop!" Jackie screamed. "What is wrong with you? You're hurting me!" She wiggled around to get out from under him, but Colton pinned her arms over her head. Seeing the dog was crazed by his actions, Colton unsnapped the leash. "Get her!" he commanded.

The dog didn't hesitate. He seized Jackie by the throat and began shaking her. Blood splattered everywhere.

Colton looked into Jackie's terrified eyes, which were closing now. She tried to speak, but only a gurgle emerged from her mouth.

The dog, frenzied by the blood, kept mauling her.

Colton saw the light fade from her eyes and felt the release he always did. He picked up a stick and waved it at the dog. "Get!" he said, but the dog was chewing on one of Jackie's arms and wouldn't stop. Bone was already visible under the flesh.

Colton decided he had to leave and ran quickly in the other direction. The dog didn't even lift his head; he was too busy ravishing what was left of Jackie's body.

Colton ran around the campus so he would be seen, then he jogged to the dorm and into his room.

Jeff was studying and barely looked up when Colton charged in. "Good run?" he asked, still reading his book.

"I didn't know the campus was so big. I'm sweating like a pig."

"Go take a shower, pal. You smell like one too."

"I'm going; I'm just going to grab a beer first." He calmly took a beer and went down the hall to the showers.

Some boys playing softball the next day found Jackie's body when the ball rolled into the woods. There wasn't much left to identify, so the EMS labeled her a Jane Doe.

The whole campus was shocked by the death. When the newspapers ran the article about Jackie, several families pulled their daughters out of the school.  The dean pleaded with the students to resume their routines, but the school remained in an uproar for several weeks.  The medical examiner concluded that she was killed by a wild animal.  Only Colton knew better.

Colton tackled like a maniac on the football field and grew popular with the student body.  He basked in the adoration he felt was his due.

## Chapter 59

Drew sent Colton a newspaper every once in a while when he thought there was something in it that would interest him. On the day one arrived, he threw it on the living room chair and forgot about it.

A few days later Jeff said, "Hey, Cutter, are you ever going to read that damn newspaper? What's that envelope shoved under the door? It has your name on it."

Colton came flying out of his room. "Oh, that rag. I don't know why Dad sent that. I might as all take a peek at it."

"What's this fancy envelope that was shoved under the door?" Jeff asked, waving the letter around.

"Gimme that!" Colton yelled and ripped it out of Jeff's hand. He tore it open and saw it was an invitation to a fraternity recruiting reception. Colton looked at Jeff with surprise. "Did you get one of these?" he asked.

"What is it?"

"An invitation to a frat reception."

"Nope, I'm not the frat type. Which one is it?"

"Phi Beta Kappa."

"Yep, you fit the bill, being a football hero. That fraternity is the hoity toity one of the bunch," he said bitterly. "No, I didn't get invited and I won't either. My father belonged, but he was kicked out because of a hazing incident."

"Why on earth did you decide to go to school here?"

"Peer pressure."

The only reason he didn't want to join the fraternity was that he liked living with Jeff and he didn't want to hurt him.

The next day at practice, the coach approached him with a big grin on his face. "I hear you're going to be a Phi Beta Kappa member."

"I haven't decided yet. My roommate is a much better candidate. He makes straight A's and is a member of the honor society."

"You'd better join, the alumni expect you to."

Colton frowned. "Do the alumni think they own me?"

"They bought you when you accepted their scholarship."

"I like to be my own person."

"Hang in there, lad. It's only for a few years. The NFL draft will take place and, unless I miss my guess, you'll be the first to go."

Colton was floored. "Do you think so?"

"Yes, I do. Now get a move on, we have a practice to start."

Colton broached the subject while he and Jeff were eating dinner.

"I don't want to join Phi Beta Kappa and leave you behind," Colton said.

"Don't worry; I'll get a new roommate. Besides, you don't have a choice, the alumni wouldn't be happy if you turned it down."

Colton walked over to Jeff and hugged him. "I'm sorry, bro," he said sadly.

Even though it was seven thirty and dark outside, Colton went to the newspaper office to think. For once, he was ashamed of his behavior and wished he was anyone but himself. Colton knew he should go somewhere for help, but if he did, he'd lose everything. He thought of Buck, the only one he had ever loved besides Patty. Now, he had lost them both. He put his head in his hands and cried.

Colton didn't want to distance himself from Jeff. He was the closest friend he had ever had.

The door quietly opened and Ted walked in. The boy's eyes were red and Colton could tell he'd been crying. "What's the matter?" he asked. "It looks like you're in as bad a shape as I am. Come on, sit down."

Ted sunk into a chair and started to cry. "I loved Jackie. She never knew it, but I worshipped the ground she walked on."

Colton spilled out the story of his not wanting to join the fraternity. The atmosphere changed abruptly. "Too bad about you and your stupid decisions!" Ted cried. "I wish I had your problems!" He got up and stormed out the door.

Colton walked slowly back to the dorm. He decided he'd take a look at the Westfield Gazette. When he opened the paper, the headline startled him. The police chief had been shot in the chest with an arrow while deer hunting. He wasn't expected to survive.

Clint Leary, a senior detective, had been appointed interim chief. Suddenly, he felt he had made a mistake when he murdered Jackie. Someone might link the murders to him because they were at the same school. "They never will," he told himself confidently. "No one's caught me yet and they never will." He crushed the paper and threw it in the trash without reading another word.

## Chapter 60

"I don't have any clothes to wear as a Phi Beta Kappa candidate. I sure as hell can't wear blue jeans!" Colton lamented to Jeff.

"Talk to the coach, he'll tell you who to call. I'm sure clothing is part of the perks you're entitled to."

Colton gave Jeff the finger, but did as he suggested and asked Coach Hogan.

He wrote down a name and a phone number and handed it to Colton. "Good luck, but I'm sure you won't need it," he said smiling.

Colton placed a call to a man named Bob Perkins in Butte, Montana.

"Saint Paul's Church," a woman answered.

"Is Mr. Perkins there?" Colton asked, thinking he had dialed the wrong number.

"Pastor Perkins is in a meeting right now, but I think they're through. Who may I say is calling?"

"Colton Colby."

"Just one moment."

Colton could hear conversation in the background and a man came on the line. "Hello, lad, I've heard great things about you. How can I help you?"

Colton told him about the recruiting reception and explained that he didn't have any clothes to wear.

"Fret no more, my son. Is there a men's clothing store around there?"

"There's Parkinson's, but it's very expensive. I can't afford to go in there."

"Don't worry, I'll call the store and open an account in your name. Buy anything you need."

"Thank you, Pastor; I can't believe my good fortune!"

"You're more than welcome, but call me Bob. Let me know if you need anything else. I'll expect a good report on your grades and keep up the good work on the football field."

Colton thanked him again and ended the conversation.

The next day he went into Parkinson's and introduced himself.

"Hello, Mr. Colby," the salesman said. "Look around and pick out anything you want. Pastor Perkins called this morning and you have unlimited credit."

Colton got back to the dorm and asked Jeff to help him unload the car. "What did you do? Buy out the store?"

Colton laughed. "Just about. Wait until you see all the great stuff I got!" He showed Jeff two sports coats, two pairs of slacks and a charcoal suit. Two silk ties were hanging around the neckline of the suit.

"Wow!" Jeff exclaimed. "Keep going. What else did you get?"

Colton showed him two cashmere sweaters and a beautiful black leather jacket.

"I could swoon," Jeff joked.

Colton showed him four shirts, one was a dress shirt and the others were casual. After that, there was a black pair of loafers and a pair of tennis shoes. He had gotten white sweat socks and black dress socks. The last package contained two sweat shirts and a denim jacket.

"Don't tell me that's all there is," Jeff mocked. "How much did all of this cost?"

"Fifteen hundred dollars," Colton replied.

"Oh my God! I'm so envious I could barf!" Jeff fell onto the sofa where he pretended to pass out.

"Cheer up, buddy. Let's go to Blanche's and have a few beers to celebrate."

"Will the alumni pay for that too?"

"I don't think so; we'll have to handle that on our own." Jeff was such a regular guy, Colton kept forgetting how rich he was.  He must have a lot of nice clothes, but he was genuinely happy for Colton.

## Chapter 61

The frat house was a grand, old brick building with two white columns in the front. Colton walked in the front door and looked around in awe. The walls were completely covered in dark wood paneling. The floor had plush tan carpeting and a winding staircase rose up to the next level.

On one wall were pictures of the alumni and Colton saw a picture of Pastor Perkins. The man had a full head of white hair and wire glasses pinched his nose. A smile lit up his face, making him look like a very nice man.

He hadn't known what to wear, so he decided on black jeans, a light blue cashmere sweater and black tennis shoes.

Colton heard footsteps behind him and turned around. A tall, red-haired member of the fraternity moved toward him, hand extended. "You must be Colton Colby," he said.

They shook hands. "Where is everybody?" Colton asked. "Am I late?"

"There are only two other recruits and they just arrived a few minutes ago. We're in the library. Come with me, I'll take you there."

The room was also paneled and contained a huge fireplace. Shelves from floor to ceiling were covered with books. Several tables and chairs were placed around for reading.

The other two candidates were sitting on the sofa. Colton was relieved to see everyone was dressed casually.

One of the boys looked at Colton and gave him a cocky grin. He recognized him as a member of the football squad. He wasn't a team player and somewhat of a hot dog, so Colton didn't like him. The other candidate was a pleasant looking boy with sandy hair and a lot of freckles.

"Welcome, Colton," a member sitting at a large oak desk said as he stood up. "I'll introduce you to the other candidates. I suspect you'll be seeing a lot of each other. This is Roy Watkins, I think you know him, Colton," he said, pointing at the football player. He pointed to the other candidate. "This is Cliff Stone. Everyone knows who you are, Colton, the star of our school's football team."

"Wait a minute," Roy interrupted. "I play tackle on the team too."

"I'm Maury Carlson, the president of this fraternity," the boy said, giving Roy a displeased look. "I'm going to give you a questionnaire to fill out. We'll leave you alone while you complete it." He motioned to the boy who had shown Colton into to room and they left together.

When they were gone, Roy looked at Colton. "Where do they get off treating you like a hot shot? Everyone knows you're a loner who doesn't have any friends except your nerdy roommate."

"Just a minute," Cliff intervened. "This is no way to start a relationship!"

Colton's made his hand into a fist, but turned his attention to the questionnaire in front of him.

When the two members walked back into the room, they sensed hostility. One of them collected the papers and announced, "Now we'll have a private interview with each of you. Please come with me, Colton."

Roy glared at him. "Naturally they'd call him first," he mumbled under his breath.

When the interviews had been completed, the two members left the room and came back fifteen minutes later. "We've decided to invite all of you to a get together with cocktails and hors d'oeuvres next Saturday night at six o'clock. You'll be further evaluated then. See you later, guys."

"How did it go?" Jeff asked.

"Fine, most of the guys I met seemed nice, but that asshole Roy Watkins' a candidate."

"Yipes, I know his parents are loaded, but everyone hates him. He must have pull somewhere.

"Let's forget about him. I'm going to the library for a while. I'll be back for our wonderful dinner. How does mac and cheese with pickles and baked beans sound?"

Jeff laughed. "Sounds delicious."

## Chapter 62

Colton could hear loud voices coming from the frat house a half a block before he got there. The house was filled with guys and girls talking to each other. Most of them had drinks in their hands.

There was a long bar set up on one side of the room. Another table held hors d'oeuvres of every description. Colton eyed a pile of boiled shrimp and his mouth watered. He was so used to hot dogs and hamburgers, the snacks looked like a feast to him.

The fireplace was lit, taking the chill out of the room.

Colton walked up to the bar, unsure what to order. He decided on a rum and coke and was just about to taste it when Cliff walked up to him.

"Quite a lay out, huh? Check out those babes!"

"Yeah, they're something else." They all looked alike to Colton. Long, straight hair, some with bangs. All of them wore too much make-up and their shirts were too short. Colton thought they looked like painted dolls. He turned to Cliff. "They're not by type," he declared.

"Me either," he replied. "I was raised on a dairy farm in Wisconsin and all the girls up there are pretty and wholesome with a minimum of make-up."

"Like a milk maid?" Colton joked.

"Exactly, they all get married young and birth little girls with rosy cheeks and blonde hair just like they have."

Bill, the fellow who led them both to the library, walked over. "Hi guys, how are you doing?"

"Fine," Cliff replied.

"Help yourself to the goodies anytime you want," he said and walked away to talk to another group.

"He's nice," Cliff commented.

"Everyone I've met here has been nice," Colton agreed.

A girl with a stemmed glass in her hand walked over to them. "Hi big guys," she said with a giggle. "I haven't seen you around here before."

"We're recruits," Cliff explained.

She took a large sip of her beverage. "Um, good. "I'm Dolly, the class slut," she said, giggling again.

She took another large drink and stumbled forward. The martini splashed all over Cliff's sports coat, leaving large splotches.

"Get me a bar towel," Colton told the bartender. He threw it to Cliff and he tried to wipe it off the best that he could.

Dolly laughed loudly and everyone looked in their direction.

"Get out of here," Colton ordered.

The drunken girl looked at him with hostility. "Make me," she said.

In one movement, Colton had her over his shoulder. He walked out the door with Dolly kicking and screaming.

"This is like a side show," one guy said loudly.

Bill went up to the bar. "Okay, boys and girls, we're closing the bar down. It's time to eat."

Moans and groans filled the room, but everyone took a plate and filled them up.

Colton returned and Bill ran up to him. "Is Dolly alright? She's a jerk, but I don't want anything to happen to her."

"Never fear, she was staggering to her sorority house when I last saw her. It's only a half a block away, so I figured she'd make it."

When Bill walked away, Colton clenched and unclenched his hands. He'd have great pleasure killing that broad. She didn't deserve to live.

"What's wrong?" Cliff asked, noticing Colton's glazed eyes.

"Nothing, I just can't stand drunken women."

"Gotcha," Cliff agreed.

Just then, there was a loud pounding on the bar and Roy shouted, "Open this fucker up! I want a drink!"

Colton and Cliff looked at each other. "He'll never make it," they said in unison.

The sweet smell of marijuana filled the air and a few couples walked up the stairs leading to the second floor.

Cliff looked at Colton and said, ""Let's get out of here."

Colton nodded and they made their way through the crowd to the door.

"Wait up, guys," Bill called. "You're in. Stop by tomorrow and I'll assign you a room."

"The hell he will," Cliff said to Colton. "I'm bailing."

When they got outside, Cliff explained he didn't need those jerks. "My family owns five hundred acres of rich farmland. We can buy and sell just about everyone in there."

Colton's face registered surprise.

"Please don't tell anyone. I just want to fit in."

"I won't," Colton said. "We'd better get back to our dorms now. I hope I'll see you around."

"You will, I come to all of the football games."

Colton started walking back to his dorm when an urgency seized him. He had to find Roy, killing him would give Colton great satisfaction.

He doubled back and found Roy slumped drunkenly over a water fountain. The sight of him made Colton's stomach turn. He kicked him in the groin and left him where he was. He knew Roy would self-destruct.

When he got back to the dorm, he walked right past Jeff and into his room. He quickly stripped off his clothes and got into bed.

Jeff poked his head in the door. "Aren't you even going to say good-night?"

"Nope," Colton said, his voice muffled by the blanket.

Jeff shook his head and shut off the lights in the living room, then went to bed himself.

When he got up in the morning, Colton was already gone. "I'd sure like to know what happened at that party," Jeff said to himself.

## Chapter 63

Colton sat on a bench in front of the dorm, hunched over to escape the cold wind. He took out his cell phone and called Pastor Perkins. "This is Colton Colby, you told me to call if I had a problem."

"Yes, my boy. What is it?"

"I know you and the rest of the alumni are going to be angry with me, but I'm not going to join the fraternity. There's no way I would fit in there. I'm not a rich kid from an important family; I'm just a good football player."

The pastor chuckled. "Son, I'm proud of you. I'll make all the necessary calls to the other alumni, but I'm sure their answer will be the same. Well, except for one," he said laughing.

"I want to thank you for all of your financial help. Without it, I couldn't have gotten this far."

"Hold on, I didn't say we were cutting you off. We'll extend the benefits until you land a job. What field do you want to pursue?"

Colton was floored. "Actually, I was thinking of becoming an English teacher."

"Then go for your PHD and become an English professor at a college. That's the only way you can make money in that field. Good luck," the pastor said and hung up the phone.

Colton sat paralyzed for a moment, not believing his good luck. Maybe this was the beginning of creating a whole new Colton. He had to hurry to make the church service before class. For once, he was looking forward to the sermon.

On his way to class, Colton passed a group of girls giggling and talking. The one in the middle had unnaturally red hair. She wore heavy make-up and a mini skirt that barely covered her rear. Seeing him watch her, she moved her hips backward and forward as if performing sex.

*You little bitch,* Colton thought. *If you were in another place, I'd off you without thinking twice.*

So much for him going down the right path. He decided he enjoyed the burning desire for release.

Colton went to football practice, glad that he had chosen to be a bad boy. When Roy charged him, he had no qualms about lowering his head and butting him hard in the stomach.

His helmet cracked several of Roy's ribs. He made a puffing sound and dropped to the ground.

Proud of himself, Colton looked at the coach and saw he was smiling.

After practice, he went to the exercise room and worked out for a while and then went back to the dorm to take a shower.

Jeff was looking in the cupboards for something to eat. "We're plum out of grub," he groused. "We'll have to hit the store again."

"That's small stuff," Colton said. "Come here, I have something to tell you."

"What is it, bro?" Jeff asked as he sat down.

"I'm not joining the fraternity. I'm going to stay right here where I belong."

Jeff took Colton's hand and pumped it. "Your old man sent you another newspaper. It's over by the door."

Colton picked it up and scanned the first page. Large headlines read "Interim Chief Ends Murder Investigation".

Colton read the article. The essence of it was, after a thorough investigation with no results, the police department had closed the case. Colton wanted to celebrate. He had won again!

## Chapter 64

Life went on as normal until Coach Hogan pulled Colton aside one day. "The Green Bay Packers drafted you in the fourth round. You'll be a damn fool if you don't take it. Sign the contract and I'll fax it to them. They want you to do a television interview too. The Packer's head office will notify you as to the channel and the date. Well done, Colton, you deserve it. You're one hell of a football player!"

Colton walked off the field in a state of bliss. He was scot free and looking forward to the future.

Was he destined to take the good road or the bad?

## About the Author

Sally A. Allen is originally from Wisconsin and currently lives in west central Florida with her Schnauzer, Sibby.

While her novels are fiction, she draws from the many experiences she's had in her life.

Visit her website at www.sally-allen.webs.com

## Other Novels by Sally A. Allen

Seeing Sparks
Fading Sparks
After the Sparks
Cougar
Choices
The Rogue
Changes
Aftermath

Cover Design by Al Mustitano
www.personalcovers.webs.com